Dear Jo

The story of losing Leah...
and searching for hope.

Dear Jo: The Story of Losing Leah ... and Searching for Hope.
Text © 2007 Christina Kilbourne

Published by Lobster Press™
1620 Sherbrooke Street West, Suites C & D
Montréal, Québec H3H 1C9
Tel. (514) 904-1100 • Fax (514) 904-1101 • www.lobsterpress.com

Publisher: Alison Fripp
Editors: Alison Fripp & Meghan Nolan
Editorial Assistants: Katie Scott & Olga Zoumboulis
Graphic Design & Production: Tammy Desnoyers
Cover Photography: Jonathon Cliff

We acknowledge the financial support of the Government of
Canada through the Book Publishing Industry Development
Program (BPIDP) for our publishing activities.

We acknowledge the support of the Canada
Council for the Arts for our publishing program.

The Canada Council | Le Conseil des Arts
for the Arts | du Canada

Library and Archives Canada Cataloguing in Publication

Kilbourne, Christina, 1967-
        Dear Jo: The story of losing Leah ... and searching for hope. /
Christina Kilbourne.

Target audience: For ages 9+.
ISBN-13: 978-1-897073-51-3
ISBN-10: 1-897073-51-8

        I. Title.

PS8571.I476D42 2007   jC813'.6   C2006-905119-4

Printed and bound in Canada.
Printed on Rolland Enviro 100 Book, 100% recycled post-consumer fibre.

In memory of Holly Jones

Acknowledgements

Special thanks to Callie Norwich and her friends at Park Avenue Public School who helped me understand twelve-year-olds when I first started thinking about this book. Thanks also to the organizers of the Muskoka Novel Marathon where Maxine first came to life. Thanks to Sam Hiyate, Jonathon Cliff, Samantha Shepperd, Mel Malton, Lisa Palmer, and Robert Morgan for their parts in helping to get this project off the ground, and especially to Meghan Nolan for her insightful suggestions and keen eye. Finally, thanks to Isabella, Leo, and Finn for being perfect models for the characters in this book.

– Christina Kilbourne

Dear Jo

The story of losing Leah...
and searching for hope.

written by
Christina Kilbourne

Lobster Press ™

November 10

Dear Diary,

Everything is black, so black I can't see through it. When it first started closing in around me, I thought I'd be okay, that I'd let it creep in a little way and then fight it back when I had the energy. The thing is, I didn't realize it was stronger than me, and now I'm afraid I won't ever win.

November 11

Dear Diary,

Happy Remembrance Day. Exactly what I needed to cheer me up – a day to remember a bunch of dead guys.

November 12

Dear Diary,

I'm *so* royally screwed up right now and it's not a good place to be. Do you know what I've been thinking about lately? Tally Hanen's cousin, Chloe. Tally was abducted from her own yard, where she was playing with Chloe. They were both five at the time. When the man grabbed Tally and started to drag her away, she yelled to Chloe to get her mom, who'd stepped inside for Popsicles. But the man shoved Tally in his car and drove away before her mother got back outside. The police were on the case in minutes. They even issued an Amber Alert. A stranger found Tally's body later that same day.

I know all this because I saw it on a TV documentary the other night. Mom would have freaked if she caught me watching it, but I couldn't turn it off once I'd started, and I couldn't sleep anyway. Now I'm having nightmares again, but not about Tally. I can't stop thinking about Chloe. I mean, it's over for Tally, she's not in the nightmare anymore. But Chloe is going to spend the rest of her life thinking that if only she'd been closer to the picket fence, she'd be the one who was abducted. That's what it's like for me right now.

November 13

Dear Diary,

It's past midnight and everyone is asleep except me, as usual. Molly is across the room snoring, and I'm under my covers with a flashlight, listening to Simple Plan on my headphones so I don't wake her. Did you ever listen to the words of *Welcome to My Life*? I swear they were writing the song for me. I think I'll switch to Avril Lavigne next, if I'm still awake.

It's pretty hard crouching under the covers and writing, but I have no choice. Mom wakes up at the slightest sound these days. So if I go anywhere, even to the bathroom, I'll have to explain to her what I'm doing up. I think she's afraid I'm going to hurt myself. I admit that I sometimes think about it, but not tonight. Tonight I'm too sad, not angry-sad which is more dangerous, just sad. I can't sleep and I have nothing to read, so I guess I'll write to you for a while. Maybe that will put me to sleep – no offense.

I actually got you many months ago, in March as a twelfth birthday present from Aunt Laurie. She thought I might want to record my thoughts and memories and, as she said in her card, preserve what it's like to be this age so I can look back when I'm an adult with kids of my own. Well, I'm not sure I will ever have kids of my own or that I want to remember this age, but maybe this will help me.

I mean, it's worth a shot. Nobody else has been able to do much. So far I've had my parents lecture me a gazillion times, I've had teachers pull me aside after school to have heart-to-hearts, I've seen the school counselor, and have even been seeing a private therapist. That's right, I'm seeing a psychiatrist, a shrink, a head doctor. I've been seeing her since the summer because Mom said I wasn't myself. I wasn't eating or going out and she was worried about some of the things I was saying, like, "I wish I was dead because I'm out of tears and can't even find relief in crying anymore."

Everyone thinks I'm psycho – even I think so at times.

November 15

Dear Diary,

I'm not sure what I'm supposed to write. I mean, what's the point of telling you everything when you can't answer back? Or really, since you're just a thing, why bother spilling my guts to you? But I promised the therapist I would try to explore some of my thoughts and feelings and not keep them bottled up. So I will. I'll just scribble in you for a while like the therapist suggested, then burn you in the fireplace.

I should probably tell you about myself, just to

get started. My name is Maxine Marie Lemay, if you can believe it. Who names a kid Maxine? Only crazed people like my parents. Mom always laughs when I complain about my name and says, "It was the hormones. They were running rampant and it seemed like a good idea at the time."

My friends call me Max, which wouldn't be so bad if everyone didn't name their pet Max. I swear, I know a hundred cats and dogs named Max and even one horse. I hate going to the park because people are always yelling out "Max!" and I twist my head around to answer, only to see some black Lab taking a poop where he's not supposed to.

I'm over five feet tall and ninety-five pounds, so I'm kind of on the skinny side. I have light brown hair, long, without bangs, that I like to wear in a ponytail. I have a few freckles, but at least they're faint.

I wear glasses and hate it when people talk about them, even though I've had them since I was three. They aren't the big Coke-bottle kind, but I would still rather not have them. Sometimes I wear contact lenses, but Mom, who is the biggest drag in the world, only lets me wear them on special occasions. I tried wearing them all the time last winter, but kept washing them down the drain by accident.

So now I mostly wear my glasses, which Leah always used to say make me look sophisticated.

Leah is my best friend, technically. Even though she's been missing almost six months, I still think of her that way. We never tell the others we're best friends, because we don't want them to feel left out, but Leah and I are like soul sisters or something. She is the most fun of all my friends and the one with the wickedest ideas about things to do, like sneaking down to the lake to go skinny dipping in the dark or spying on the high school boys at track practice. The only problem with Leah is that she has to be the best at everything. She has to be the fastest, the smartest, the funniest, the bravest, the cutest. I guess it's because she's an only child and is used to coming first all the time.

When I think about Leah, I ache all over and want out of my body, just to stop the pain. Everyone tells me I need to put it out of my mind, but I can't stop thinking about her, not even for a minute, not even if I wanted to. She's always with me. When I try to do something else, she hovers on the edge of my vision and she's always in my dreams, the same haunting dream over and over. That's why I am afraid to fall asleep at night.

November 16

Dear Diary,

I know I should write more about Leah, but I don't have the energy today, so I'm going to tell you about me instead. I have a little sister and a little brother, and both of them are a pain in the butt. I'm not allowed to say that out loud, but I guess that's what diaries are for. Molly is my little sister. She's five and she's adorable, really. Even when I hate her, I can't help but think she's adorable. One day when Aunt Laurie asked her what she wanted to be when she grew up, she said, "Maxine." That made me feel good. She has cute blue eyes and long blond hair that falls into the most perfect ringlets. She's not bad for a five-year-old, but it gets really annoying that she wants to do *everything* I do all the time. If I'm reading, she wants to read, if I watch TV, she wants to watch TV, if I go to the park, she wants to tag along. And I usually have to take her. Except that lately, I haven't wanted to go anywhere. I can't even escape by going to my bedroom because we have to share one, which I think is ridiculous.

My little brother is almost two. If I think I have a bad name, he's got it worse because his name is Gus. Nobody names a kid Gus. Except Mom and Dad, of course, who must have forgotten what it's like to have a weird name in the school yard. Talk about being a target for abuse. Good thing Gus is tough, because he's going to get picked on a lot. He also has red hair, which makes him stick out even more. And you can bet he'll end up with freckles too. The red hair and freckles came from our grandfather. Mom says we are her "Neapolitan ice cream" children because we all have a different color of hair: mine is brown, Molly's is blond, and Gus's is red. Strangers always ask if we're all from the same father, which really annoys Dad. Of course, it would help if Molly called them Mom and Dad instead of by their first names, Debbie and Wayne. But that's a whole other story.

We live in Port Hope, which is a small town. So if we need to go somewhere for something special, like Dad's computer supplies or the new china cabinet we got last year, we go to the city where Aunt Laurie lives. It's only about an hour and a half away, the way my dad drives. I used to wish we lived closer to the city, but now I wish we lived farther away, ten hours away, one hundred hours away. Maybe if Port Hope was farther from the city, Leah would still be here and I wouldn't be inside writing to you on what appears to be a beautiful fall day.

I don't actually know it's a beautiful fall day because I haven't been out. I refuse to go anywhere these days, unless it's to school. I hate going there too, but I don't have a choice since Mom and Dad make me go. School is the worst place to be because everyone stares at me all the time, and I'm afraid they're blaming me for what happened to Leah. But I'll write more about that later.

Mom just came in and told me they were going to rake the yard so that Molly and Gus can play in the leaves. She came in with her coat on and said, "Maxine, would you like to come too? It's a gorgeous day out there!"

"Nah, I'm going to keep writing. Maybe later." I didn't even look up at her.

"Gus and Molly really want you to come."

"No, really, that's okay. I'm in the middle of this."

"Suit yourself. We'll be in the back if you need us."

Normally she would have dragged me outside for fresh air, but my therapist now has her convinced I need time to write. Maybe having a diary isn't so bad after all.

November 18

Dear Diary,

I hate to say it, but I think it's kind of childish to keep a diary, so I've decided to keep a journal instead. I'm going to call you Jo, for short. And I'm going to start again, on a fresh page.

November 18

Dear Jo,

I looked back at what I've written and realized I never told you anything about my other friends. I do have other friends, besides Leah, but right now I'm not much in the mood for seeing them. I haven't even told you much about Leah, really. But that is going to take some time. So you'll have to be patient. I have five main friends and we do everything together, or we did until Leah went missing. We met in kindergarten and have been friends ever since. Their names are Leah, Lexi, Emma, Kelsey, and Amanda. See how ridiculous Maxine sounds now? Leah used to tell me I could change my name when I got older. But Mom told me I'd have to wait until I'm eighteen and that's another five years or so away.

Lexi, Emma, and I all live in the same neighborhood in Port Hope. It's a neighborhood of mostly older houses that have been fixed up and added onto. Our house is one of the oldest in Port Hope, and we even have an old carriage house out back with an apartment up top that we rent to a young couple who just got married. Our house has two main floors, a scary basement, and a walk-up attic full of dusty boxes. I like it up there, but it gets too hot in the summer and too cold in the winter. We are only six blocks from the main street of Port Hope and across town from Lost Lake Park, where we go swimming in the summer. Port Hope is a really good place to live in the summer because of the lakes.

Kelsey lives outside of town in the country, which is a drag because it's too far to get to by bike, but cool because she has a horse and I get to ride him when I stay overnight. Amanda lives out of town too, but just a little way, on Loon Lake in a really, really nice house. Mom says Amanda's family is "Very fortunate," but Dad puts it more like, "They have money coming out the wahzoo." I never say that to Amanda though. Her father sells houses, which must be better for making money than fixing computers like Dad does.

Leah's house is on the west side of Port Hope, in a neighborhood behind the high school. I used to spend a lot of time over there. But now I never go except to drop off a card or light a candle. I'm afraid of seeing her parents again. I can't stand to see how much they've changed since Leah disappeared. I can't stand to see how sad they are. We used to go over there to use the internet because Leah's parents had it and mine didn't. My parents said it was dangerous and that we were too young and could get in trouble, but we didn't believe them and we didn't listen.

Of course, Leah was the first one of us who found Habbo Hotel on the internet. I remember the first day we ever went there. It was just after my birthday and there had been a huge snow storm. All the schools in Port Hope were closed. Mom called in sick to work so she could stay home with us. We had a pretty fun day. We got to watch cartoons and stay in our pajamas for most of the morning. I was so happy about not having to go to school, I didn't even complain about having to watch PBS Kids, except for when *Teletubbies* came on. Even Molly hates *Teletubbies*. But Gus loves it, and that day he sat and stared at it the whole time it was on, which was better than having him climb all over me. He has very sharp elbows that always end up in my ribs. If you've ever had kid elbows and knees jammed into your side, you know how much it hurts.

Mom let us make chocolate chip cookies after lunch that day, and then Molly and I went outside and made a snow fort with a tunnel and windows and two separate rooms. It took us forever to make, and when we came back in we ate the warm cookies and drank glasses of cold milk. When Gus went for a nap, we got to watch Nickelodeon instead of PBS Kids and *SpongeBob SquarePants* was on. That's my second favorite show, next to *Malcolm in the Middle*.

In the afternoon, Leah called and invited me over, so I went to her house. I was exhausted when I got there because I had to walk through snow up to my knees. The plow hadn't been by yet. We logged onto Habbo Hotel and I thought it was really cool. It's a virtual hotel and you pick a character and can go all over and talk to other guests or go swimming or order food and drinks from the bar. Leah, Lexi, and Amanda were total Habbos. They used to go there at night and talk to each other, and then they'd talk about it at school the whole next day, which made me feel left out. But that snow day, I had Leah and the internet all to myself, and we had a lot of fun. I came home wanting the internet more than ever.

Once I get something in my mind, I can't let it go.

November 20

Dear Jo,

Gus started saying my name. It comes out more like "Zine," as in magazine, than Maxine, but at least he says something. He doesn't say anything for Molly or Mom or Dad. Mom says his speech is slow, but he's pretty smart.

Right now his favorite game is "up and down and around." He invented it himself. He pulls me by my hand to the middle of the floor and falls on the ground. Then I'm supposed to do the same. Then he pulls me up off the ground and we spin around until we get dizzy and fall down again. Then we do it over. It's cute and it made me smile for a little while. But then I felt really tired and came to write instead. The last thing I was telling you about was our internet phase.

If I try to pinpoint when our whole internet craze started, I'd have to say it was in March, right about the time I found out I was going to have to get braces. I was really bummed out about that. I mean, I figured I was already ugly enough with my freckles and glasses. The day I found out, I was crying, and Dad came into my room. He asked me if he could do anything to make me feel better. So I said that I'd like to get the internet and he looked sort of tired and said, "Maxine, we've been through this before."

"I know, but all my friends go online at night and chat and I get left out and it's making me lose friends."

"If your friends don't like you because you aren't online, then they aren't very good friends, are they?"

"They're the best ones I've got right now and besides, I like them."

"If they're really your friends, they'll like you if you're online or not."

"But *everyone* is online except me. Even Kelsey, who lives out in the country, in the middle of nowhere, is on dial-up."

"I'm sorry you're disappointed, but you know what Mom says."

"Yeah, that she doesn't care what other parents let their kids do, she's only responsible for her own kids. I hate that word. *Responsible*." I made a face to emphasize my point.

"I know, but it's true what she says about the internet. It can be dangerous."

"I know. There're predators and pornography, even con artists trying to get you to give out your personal information so they can steal your identity."

"I'm sure it's hard for you to understand."

"I'm not stupid. I know not to give out my real name or address and not to agree to meet anyone in person."

"There's more to it than that. Besides, Maxine, you're only twelve. When you get a little older, we can discuss it again."

After that I knew there was no way I was ever going to get the internet. I'd given it my best shot. So I went to Leah's house more and more, and we started going to more and more places on the internet. We even met people online. At the time I thought this was the most fun I'd ever had with Leah, but now I remember different things about her.

Like just now, for no reason, I remembered the day she learned to do a back flip off the dock at Lost Lake Park. She saw one of the high school boys do it, and when they left, she spent the rest of the afternoon trying it herself. She scraped her shin and almost cracked her head open on the dock, but she wouldn't quit. Even when I begged to go home because I was getting sunburned, she kept trying until she could do it perfectly. Then she made us go back the next day. She waited until those same boys came by and she did five in a row. She acted like this was something she'd been doing all her life.

This is the worst part of my day: when I'm lying in bed at night, like right now, trying to sleep. I can't stop myself from remembering her and all the crazy things we've done together. Then I try to feel her, wherever she is. I try with all my energy to send her thoughts so she will feel me thinking about her and won't feel so alone. Some nights I swear I can feel her out there, her heart beating, her chest rising, her pulse racing.

November 21

Dear Jo,

Gus turned two today. Mom had balloons and cake, and Molly insisted on setting a place at the table for her imaginary friend, Georgia. I hate Molly's imaginary friends because she insists I talk to them, and I hate talking to thin air. There were a lot of presents, considering he's just a baby. Molly used her allowance and bought him a family of plastic whales that squirt water for the bathtub. He thought that was fun. I should have bought him something too. We didn't have any other kids over because Mom said he wouldn't notice the difference. We spent the whole night with him and his new toys, until he had to go to bed. His favorite thing all night was bouncing the balloons. Now both Molly and Gus are tucked into bed, and I am at the kitchen table where Mom can keep an eye on me while I do my homework.

I'm supposed to be studying for an English test, but I can't be bothered. I'm already failing, so what's the point? It's not like I'm stupid. I used to get straight As until this year, and I used to be allowed to do my homework whenever and wherever I wanted. But now my parents don't trust me. I guess I wouldn't either if I were them. I mean, I went from being an honors student to failing all my subjects. I went from being trustworthy and *responsible* to almost getting myself killed. See how everything takes me back to the internet and Leah? And people tell me I should try and put her out of my mind.

The internet almost became an addiction for Leah and me. After we got bored with Habbo Hotel, we started to go to music forums where we could chat online with other people who like the same music as we do. We spent a lot of time at Avril Lavigne's fan club site where there were forums on everything to do with Avril. We thought it was so awesome, especially the ones that discussed her upcoming concerts. One night we met a really cool guy there who called himself "2funE." He said he was sixteen and lived in the city where Aunt Laurie lives. We didn't think he was really sixteen because his spelling was awful, but he was hilarious and had us ROTFL in no time. Leah and I pretended to be one person, "hottietoo," and gave the age fourteen, but didn't give a location.

After we met him on the fan club site a few times, he said we should exchange e-mail addresses so we could write back and forth in private. He said we could even leave bedtime messages that way. So Leah and I went to MSN, got a Hotmail account with the same name, and agreed to keep pretending to be one person. Of course, I couldn't log on for bedtime messages, but Leah could and she would call and read them to me. And she promised not to answer any e-mails or instant messages without calling me first to get my input.

Mom doesn't know, but I kept some of 2funE's e-mails. Some of them Leah printed and brought to me, and some I printed at school, once I started writing 2funE on my own from the computer room. Maybe I'll burn them one day. Maybe I'll have a big bonfire and burn this journal and all of those e-mails, and the memories will burn away too. Maybe then I'll be free.

November 24

Dear Jo,

I got out of school early today because Mom took me to get my braces on. I've been dreading it for eight months and it's as bad as I thought it would be. Now I'm an official metal-mouth. I told the orthodontist I didn't really care which color of elastics he used, but he told me I had to pick, so now I have blue on top and purple on the bottom. Lexi came by after dinner to see them and laughed. I didn't even want her to come over in the first place, but she showed up anyway. I hate her for laughing at me when I feel so miserable. That was one of the things I liked about 2funE. He never made fun of me, the way Lexi does, and he always made me feel important. I don't know why I ended up keeping this e-mail, but it shows how focused he became on me, which made me want to keep his attention even more.

> Hey Hottietoo GF. You are so cool and so funny and I can just tell from the way you write that you are smart and pretty too. Only pretty girls have a

sense of humor like you. I liked hearing about what you and your freinds did last weekend. They sound really cool. Maybe when we get to know each other better I can get to know them too. I went to my freind's party last night and met a real QT. She wanted to sit on my lap, but I couldn't let her because all I could think about was you. Now I am going to bed and I'm going to fall asleep with you on my mind. I hope you do the same. GTG. TOY. 2funE

November 25

Dear Jo,

Nobody told me braces would hurt. I just about collapsed this morning when I took a bite of my toast. Every single tooth shot with pain. It brought tears to my eyes. Mom saw I was crying and made a big fuss over me, which made me feel worse. Then she made me a yogurt smoothie for breakfast and packed pudding cups in my lunch. She told me if I needed to come home early, to have the office call her and she'd come get me right away. Even Molly tried to cheer me up by giving me her favorite Barbie to take to school.

When I saw Emma she said I looked good with braces and that Lexi was just jealous that I was going to have perfectly straight teeth and hers were crooked. Of course she didn't say that in front of Lexi. Needless to say, the whole rest of the day was a drag and nothing good happened. It's hard to act happy when your best friend is missing and your mouth aches.

All I've wanted to do since breakfast is come home and go to bed. So here I am, finally. Mom brought me home the new Harry Potter book to read, but I wanted to write a little bit first. Maybe the therapist has a point, or maybe not. But I'm starting to like this journal writing thing. It's like having a secret friend who doesn't judge you. Maybe that's why I liked writing to 2funE. He was easy to write to and he was easy to get along with. He liked all the same things as me, like gummy worms and *Shrek*. His favourite TV shows were *SpongeBob SquarePants* and *Malcolm in the Middle*, just like me. He told me he had two little brothers that he had to put up with all the time and they were a pain in the a--! I thought he was *sooooo* bad. I made a bet with Leah that he used swearwords in person when there were no adults around. I could just tell that about him. But I thought he was really sweet and I loved getting his e-mails. Even though he was writing to hottietoo, which was technically both Leah and me, it felt like he was writing only to me. Leah liked him too, she said, but she was more interested in some other guy she met named "muscleboy". So eventually, I took over being hottietoo by myself and 2funE never knew the difference.

The thing I liked best about 2funE was that he understood what it was like to have old-fashioned parents and little kids around who wrecked his stuff. None of my other friends can understand because they don't have anyone younger in their families. And he gave me really good advice too. Like this:

> Hey Hottietoo GF. How R U? Don't let your parents get you down about your curfew. Your right and eight o-clock is way too early for someone your age, but parents have to be more careful these days, at least thats what mine are always saying to me. I think thats part of the problem with being the oldest, parents forget your not a little kid. The

best way to get along with parents is to let them think their getting their own way. So don't make a big fight with them about this. It's better to slip uner the radar as much as possible, like they do on Survivor. MTF. TOY.

When I read this now, I see how he was trying to get between me and my parents. But at the time, I thought he was just a really nice guy reaching out to me. I thought he liked me for being me. I was such a fool.

November 26

Dear Jo,

Gus has discovered how to pick his nose. Now that's all he does. He's always got his finger up there digging around for something. Then he eats it. I told Mom it was really gross to watch and could she please tell him to stop, but she gave me that "don't be ridiculous" look and said, "don't look if it bothers you." I wasn't sure what she thought I was being ridiculous about, but I didn't take a chance on getting a lecture by asking. So then I asked if she could ask him not to do it when my friends are over because they already think I have a weird enough family, and she gave me her exasperated look and said, "I wish it was that easy." I swear she doesn't listen to what I'm saying. I guess that's why I'm hiding in my room writing to you. I never thought about this until right now, but maybe you are helping me fill two gaps – Leah and 2funE.

Sometimes, if I couldn't get over to Leah's and write 2funE a bedtime message, I'd dictate it to her over the phone. It felt a bit weird once we got more serious, letting her see what we said to each other, but it was my only option. So we went back and forth like that for weeks with Leah as the invisible go-between. I never suspected things were just as serious with her and muscleboy, but I guess I should have because she no longer seemed to care about my messages to 2funE.

Eventually we told the others about 2funE and muscleboy, and sometimes I would let them see one of 2funE's e-mails, and we would all compose a reply together. I felt a little guilty doing that, like I was lying to him, but then the others said I was already lying about my age, which was true. Sometimes we wrote such funny e-mails that I would just about

PMP (pee my pants) and we would be SWL (screaming with laughter). I did the typing, since I was officially hottietoo by then, which meant I got to use the best ideas and ignore the rest. I never stopped to wonder why we didn't see muscleboy's e-mails or why we didn't all write one together for Leah. But I see now I should have wondered.

November 27

Dear Jo,

Tonight at dinner Molly asked, "Can I take my bones with me when I go to heaven?" Mom and Dad just about choked on their meatloaf (yuck!) because they thought it was such a bizarre thing to ask. Poor Molly. Mom and Dad didn't look like they were ever going to answer, so I said, "No, you don't get to take your bones or teeth or skin or blood or hair or anything. You turn into a ghost and just float up to heaven."

"Does that mean I can't take my velvet dress?" she asked. She was upset because she loves her velvet dress and wears it about four days a week. Sometimes Mom sneaks into our room at night, takes it and washes it, then returns it by morning, just so Molly won't freak out about having to wear a different dress, or worse, pants!

So I said, "No, you can't take any clothes or toys. But don't worry, because you won't need them in heaven. God has way better toys than we do."

"Like what?"

"Like Barbies that really talk and move and dress themselves," I lied, just so she wouldn't get upset and annoy me all night.

"That would be cool," she said.

That was the end of the conversation. She was satisfied. Mom and Dad stared at me as if I was crazy ... or brilliant. I couldn't tell which. But I knew I had to set Molly straight or she would go on and on about it for weeks. She's like that and so am I. Once we get onto something, we just won't let it go. I guess that's why I couldn't stop writing to 2funE, even though I knew it was wrong and that my parents would ground me forever if they found out. In fact, I know I shouldn't ever admit this, that if I did my parents would freak out, I mean FREAK OUT in a big, huge disastrous way, but I loved 2funE. Of course, I don't anymore, I don't even believe in love, but I really truly did back then. It got so that we'd write several times a day. I'd rush to school early in the morning to check for an e-mail from him, write him one, then check again at lunch and after school. I never even wondered where he was writing from or whose computer he was using. There was so much I didn't ask or think to ask, not that asking would have mattered. Lying over the internet is just too easy. You can't tell what is the truth and what is a lie when there are only words on a screen. I guess that's why my parents thought it was so dangerous.

November 28

Dear Jo,

I've had it with sharing a room. I can't have the light on after 8:00 p.m. or have my music playing. It's totally annoying. And besides, I'm getting tired of Molly getting into my things all the time. So tonight at dinner, I asked if I could get my own room. Here's how the conversation went.

Me: "Can I have my own bedroom?"

Dad: "Why?"

Me: "Because I'm twelve and I don't want to share with a five-year-old anymore."

Mom: "There aren't any spare rooms."

Me: "Molly and Gus could share. They're closer in age."

Mom: "Gus won't sleep with someone else in the room, you know that."

Me: "I could move into the office and Dad could set up the office downstairs."

Dad: "There's no phone line downstairs."

Me: "Then I could have my *bedroom* downstairs."

Mom: "You'd be too far away from us."

Me: "That's the point."

Dad: "It's pretty damp down there."

Me: "I don't mind. I could use the dehumidifier."

Mom: "You wouldn't be afraid of spiders?"

Me: "No."

Dad: "Or rats?"

Me: "No."

Mom: "Or monsters?"

Me: "No, of course not."

Molly: "But I like having you in my room. I'd miss you too much if you went downstairs."

Me: "You'd have more space to yourself and I could leave some of my Beanie Babies to keep you company."

Molly: "Really?"

Me: "Sure."

Molly: "Okay."

Me back to Mom and Dad: "So?"

Dad: "We'll think about it. Give us some time to see if we can work it out."

Me: "How much time?"

Dad: "I don't know. Two weeks?"

Me: "It's a deal."

So, it wasn't a "yes," but it wasn't a "no" either. At least they said they would think about it, which gives me a 50/50 chance. I thought of telling them it would give me more privacy to write in my journal, or lying and telling them the therapist suggested I need my own space, but right now I can't stomach lying. Besides, I think they're probably in touch with the therapist, so I'd be caught in a second. I wish I'd worried more about being caught earlier in the year when I was so wrapped up in 2funE. Then maybe things would be different now. Maybe I would have been able to keep Leah safe.

It always comes back to 2funE for me. He's my worst nightmare. But still, despite the fact that he's my enemy, I have the last e-mail I ever got from him. I must have read it 500 times and it made my heart leap every time. Now it makes me feel like puking.

> Hey Hottietoo GF. How's my sweet thing? I am so crazy about you I just have to suggest a crazy idea. Why don't we meet? I know they say you aren't supposed to meet up with strangers from the internet, but we're not strangers any more. I feel like I know you better than anyone in the world and I just want to see if we connect as well in real life. What about meeting at the Milltown Mall? I can meet you any time. I'd even skip school to meet you. Think about how sweet it would be to have a real date. Maybe we could go see a movie and hold hands in the dark. It makes me shiver just to think about it. I know you might have to take some time to think about this, but I will go mental if I don't meet you soon. Carpe diem, sieze the day. We have to meet, to find some way. I will wait nervusly for your answer. I think I love you. TOYA.

I never got to make plans to meet 2funE because when I got home from school that day, I got in huge trouble. My parents grounded me, which meant I was prevented from absolutely everything to do with computers and from going out. I guess that was the lucky part for me.

November 30

Dear Jo,

My first mistake, or perhaps it wasn't a mistake after all, but the reason I finally got caught writing to 2funE was that Mom found an e-mail from him in the pocket of my jeans when she was doing the laundry. I left it there by accident, after Gus spilled his juice on me and I had to change quickly before school. 2funE said I should never print them, but I had such a good hiding place that I wasn't worried. And besides, I liked to read them before bed. When Mom found it, she freaked out completely. She said that was exactly the reason she didn't get me the internet in the first place, that she had trusted me and I had broken that trust. She said I wasn't allowed over to anyone's house until I could prove I was mature enough to handle the freedom. Then she sent me to my room and about an hour later, she came up with Dad and they both had those awful, disappointed looks on their faces. I got the whole "internet-predator-you-have-to-learn-how-to-be-responsible" lecture again. She must have used the word "responsible" a hundred times.

When they left, Mom called Leah's mother, so Leah got in trouble too. I was afraid I wouldn't have a single friend at school the next day. I thought it was going to be the worst day of my life. Now that I'm looking back, though, I realize I had no idea what the worst day could be. Maybe I still don't and that's what really scares me.

As it turned out, Leah was grounded too, but she didn't hate me, which was a huge relief because if she did, I knew Lexi, Amanda, Emma, and Kelsey would be sure to hate me too. They always copy Leah. She said her mom wasn't really mad and was just upset because she'd been writing to a high school boy she didn't even know. I was pretty hard on myself about the whole thing, but Leah said, "Hey, at least we're both grounded and missing all the fun at the same time." She always had a way of looking at the bright side of things.

Leah wasn't allowed out at night or on the

weekends for two weeks. That was her parents' version of being grounded. My parents' version of being grounded meant I wasn't allowed to go to anyone's house, watch TV, or talk on the phone for two weeks. Plus, Mom called the school to say I wasn't allowed in the computer room anymore, which meant I couldn't even write to 2funE. Leah was still allowed on the computer because her parents were pretty clueless about the internet, so she said she'd log on to Hotmail as hottietoo and tell him she was going on a family holiday, that she would write when she got back in a few weeks. I knew it wasn't a permanent solution, but it bought me time to think of something else, so I agreed.

All that time, I was stuck at home doing homework, playing with Molly and Gus, and missing 2funE. Luckily I like to read, so I read a lot. The first book I read was *Hanna's Suitcase*, which was amazing. I couldn't put it down. Mom looked pleased to see me reading, and Dad said it would do me good to spend more time with my nose in a book instead of on the internet. He works on computers all the time at work so he doesn't like to have to see them when he comes home. I liked the book because Hanna sounded brave. I was so sad when she died that I cried and cried, though secretly I was crying for 2funE. I was such a baby back then. I'd never cry over a stupid boy or a stupid book now, even if it was a true story. Now I have real things to cry about, but I don't have any tears left.

After that, Mom found me an old copy of *The Diary of Anne Frank*, which was really cool, now that I think back, because it was all written in journal entries! If I don't burn this journal eventually, someone could find it and publish it. Of course, I'd have to die for that to happen.

I tried not to mope around the house because I didn't want Mom to think I'd fallen for this guy. She was mad and she hadn't even read one of the really serious e-mails. But the truth was I felt as if my heart was breaking and I worried about how 2funE was feeling. I knew he would be waiting and waiting for me to get back from vacation and wouldn't under-stand why I didn't ever write back. I was afraid he'd think I forgotten him or didn't like him anymore. So even though it was a huge risk, I made plans to go to Leah's house when I got un-grounded so I could use her computer. I knew I had to write one last time to tell him I could never write to him again and why. But I never got the chance.

December 1

Dear Jo,

Molly lost her first tooth today. She was mortified even though I told her it was normal and reminded her of all the teeth I'd lost. But I couldn't comfort her no matter what I said.

She said, "What if I keep falling apart?"

"You're not falling apart," I told her. "You just lost one tooth."

"But I could lose more like you. Then I could lose my hair like Dad, and then what if my skin falls off the way it does for snakes? Then I won't be left with anything but bones and they'll fall apart. Then I'll float up to heaven the way you said would happen!"

"But, Molly," I said, "see how all my teeth grew back?" I opened my mouth to show her, but forgot about my braces and that upset her more.

"But they had to wire yours together. Maybe they'll have to wire me together too!"

It was really hard not to laugh at the look on her face, but I finally convinced her she wasn't falling apart and suggested Dad could make her a necklace with her tooth. So, after dinner, Dad wrapped her tooth with wire and threaded it onto an old silver chain of mine, and she put it around her neck and said she was going to keep it forever and take it for show-and-tell. I told her she wouldn't get any money from the tooth fairy if she didn't leave it under her pillow, but she said she'd rather have her tooth in case a new one didn't come in and she had to glue the old one back.

I wonder if I could dismantle myself that way, if I could take myself apart, piece by piece and then float away. It sounds like such a relief. Of course, that is just between you and me. I would never say that out loud to anyone. Mom and Dad would freak if they heard me utter such a thought and even Lexi or Emma would get that ghostly look on their faces like I was officially nuts. And the therapist, boy would she have a field day with something like that! Speaking of the therapist, I should probably get back to exploring my feelings some more, which brings me back to Leah.

All the time while we were grounded, Leah continued to write to muscleboy and I was really jealous. It seemed so unfair that I had to give up 2funE and she didn't have to give up her internet BF. And she still wouldn't say much about muscleboy, even when I asked, which made me even more upset with her. So, just to make her mad too, I told her about 2funE's suggestion to meet and that he said he thought he was in love with me. She got really agitated then. She told me I should tell him the truth, that I didn't live anywhere near the city and that I wasn't really fourteen. I told her there was no way I could do that and she told me I should break it off, that it was getting too serious. I couldn't believe what she was suggesting and I accused her of being jealous because 2funE liked me better than muscleboy liked her. Then she laughed at me and said I had no idea about anything, especially not about love and boys. That made me really *really* angry and I knew she just wanted to be first again at everything like she always does.

We didn't talk to each other for *six* days after that. She didn't call me and I didn't call her. Even at school she avoided me and because she wasn't talking to me, the others tried not to talk to me either. That meant I was stuck without any friends and without a way to write to 2funE. It was the only fight we ever had and I still don't know what made her so mad. Maybe I never will, but I still worry that our fight made her go running right into muscleboy's arms.

December 2

Dear Jo,

The last time I saw Leah was when Emma invited her, Lexi, and me to the drive-in. It was just after we were both finished being grounded and had started talking again, but I could still feel the tension between us. We went in the van with Emma's parents. I noticed right away that Leah was being quiet that night, and not just to me. She wasn't acting sad or angry, just distracted and like we were all getting on her nerves. She sometimes acted like she was older and smarter than us, which she wasn't, so we never thought much of it.

It was the opening weekend of the drive-in, which meant it was a "dusk-to-dawn" show and was packed with people. We got there early so we could get a good spot, but by the time it was dark, there were cars parking along the fence. Emma's dad parked backward. We opened the back doors of the van and stretched out on the floor with lots of pillows and blankets as if we were camping. Emma's parents sat in front of the van in lawn chairs and mostly ignored us. We had a whole cooler of pop, bags of popcorn, Cheezies, and gummy worms. We ate until we couldn't eat another bite. After the first movie, we whispered about 2funE.

Lexi said, "I wish I could meet a boyfriend online."

"I guess you just have to keep trying," I said, feeling grown-up.

"Maybe I could write to 2funE as hottietoo, since you aren't allowed to write him anymore."

"I don't think so," I said, and I felt that jealous churning in my stomach. "He knows me too well by now. He'd know you weren't me."

"Well, he's just going to find someone else if you don't write him. So maybe I'll just write him as myself," Lexi said hotly.

"No he won't find someone else. He loves me," I said.

Then, to change the topic, because Lexi was really starting to bug me, I asked Leah about muscleboy.

She laughed, flipped her hair, and said, "I'm getting tired of all this baby talk. Let's go pee before I burst."

Then she climbed out of the van and we scrambled after her.

At the concession stand, when we were waiting outside the bathroom for Leah to come out, I said to the others, "It's weird, Leah never tells us anything about muscleboy."

"Maybe he doesn't really exist. Maybe she made him up," Lexi suggested.

"Yeah, maybe she could tell you were the one 2funE really liked so she let you have him and just invented muscleboy to save face," Emma said.

"Maybe," I said as I considered the possibility. But still, it didn't seem likely to me.

We didn't stay for the last three movies, which was okay because I was almost asleep by the end of the second one and I'd already seen all of them when they first came out at the theater.

Lexi was first to be dropped off. Her mother turned on the outside lights when we pulled in the driveway, then met her at the door. Lexi rolled her eyes when she saw her mother waiting in a robe and we laughed.

We dropped Leah off second, and Emma's father idled in the driveway until we saw her unlock and open the front door. He said he wanted to be sure she got in safely. Just as she stepped inside, she turned to wave goodnight and threw us a huge smile, like she just won the lottery or something. Then we pulled out of the driveway and drove to my house.

The next day, when Leah didn't turn up for our soccer game, Emma and I thought it was weird. I mean, we'd just seen her the night before, and she was fine. But then we figured maybe she was tired from being out late and slept in.

I remember every single minute from that game. We lost to the Lakers 4 - 2. I got the second goal, and a girl from the other team got the ball in her face and left the field with a bloody nose. Molly sat on the sidelines with her plastic megaphone and yelled, "Go, Maxine, Go," and everyone thought she was hilarious, even Emma, who usually says she's a pest. Dad called her Megaphone Molly for the rest of the day.

Even to this day, I haven't seen Leah, not since we dropped her off at her house after the drive-in. I still can't believe it actually, even though it's been six-and-a-half months. I keep expecting her to call or come over or be at school when I get there. I can't believe she just disappeared.

It's funny how clear those two days are in my memory, and it's infuriating too. Because no matter how many times I go over the hours and minutes, I can't recall a single clue to tell me where she might be.

December 3

Dear Jo,

When I got home from school the Monday after the soccer game, Mom was crying. I could tell she was trying to keep herself together, but her eyes were swollen and red and her nose was raw from blowing it so much. She'd left work early and picked up Gus and Molly from day care. I was surprised to find them there already because they didn't usually get home until just before dinner.

It was really creepy, and I will never forget what it felt like when my whole world collapsed in two minutes.

Mom told me to sit down. She was moving really slow and deliberate as if she was sick, and I started getting edgy. I knew there was nothing I could be getting in big trouble for. I hadn't had a chance to write back to 2funE, even though I hadn't stopped thinking about him for a minute.

Finally she sat down and took my hands in hers. I could feel the tremble in her, and it made me start to shiver. She said, "Sweetheart, something terrible has happened."

"Is Dad okay?" I started to panic.

"Dad's fine. Everyone in our family is fine. But sweetheart, Leah is missing."

"I know. She must be sick or something because she wasn't at soccer Saturday or at school today."

I think I knew what Mom was saying, but my brain refused to believe it. I mean, I'd wondered why Leah hadn't called when we talked to each other on the phone at least once a day, but I assumed it was because we were still kind of fighting.

"No, she's not sick. She's missing. The police are looking for her."

"Looking where?" I asked. My stomach was starting to heave.

"Everywhere. All around town. They've put together a search party. Dad's been there all day."

"He didn't go to work?"

"No."

"When did you find out?"

"Leah's parents called this morning after you left for school."

"Why didn't you get me? I could have looked too. And Emma and Lexi and Kelsey and Amanda."

"We didn't want to upset you. Or alarm you. We were hoping we'd find her by now, that there was a misunderstanding or something, that she was with one of her friends."

"But I'm her best friend."

"I know."

"Where do they think she is?"

"They aren't sure. But they want to talk to you and see if you have any ideas."

That night, the police came over to our house and we talked for a long time about the evening of the drive-in and how Leah had been acting lately, if she had said or done anything strange or unusual. I said I didn't remember anything, but then I remembered that smile of hers when she was going into her house. We talked about what we liked to do in our spare time and, of course, they wanted to know where we went on the internet. I told them about Habbo Hotel and the music forums we liked to visit. I told them about meeting 2funE and muscleboy online. I felt really uncomfortable talking to them about 2funE, and they asked the most personal questions about what he said to me. They asked me if he ever suggested we meet, and I didn't know whether to lie or not. In the end I told them the truth.

They wanted to see his e-mails and I told the officers that most of them were saved on Leah's computer and the rest were in my Hotmail account. Then they took me over to Leah's house so I could help them log on to her computer. Of course, Mom wanted to come with me, but the police officer assured her they would take good care of me and that the fewer people they took over to Leah's house, the better it would be for her parents. Speaking of Mom, I've got to sign off now. It's lights out, as usual, and I don't have the energy to argue with her tonight.

December 4

Dear Jo,

It rained all night, so when we woke up today, Molly's snowman was a soggy mushy puddle in the backyard. She was so disappointed, she started to cry. I let her play with my Beanie Babies and that cheered her up. But when I got home from school, she'd left all of them on the floor and Gus was chewing on my new blue Sherbert The Bear. I couldn't believe it. I was so mad I ripped it out of his hand and he started to cry. Sherbert The Bear was

Leah's favorite of all the Beanie Babies, that's why I took my original to her house to add to all the candles and flowers people were leaving during the summer. Anyhow, Mom came running to see what was the matter and said, "Maxine, calm down! He doesn't know any better, he's just a baby."

But that made me madder and I said, "He'd know better if someone taught him better. Look at this, he almost chewed the ear off. We'd be better off with a dog!"

Then Mom said, "Maxine!" really sharp-like, Gus ran out into the hallway, and I slammed my door in her face. Gus started to cry harder. I hate having a little sister who never puts my stuff away and a little brother who eats it and parents who don't know a thing about what it's like to be me.

Anyhow, that's just to let you know what kind of day I've been having. I also got into a fight with my therapist because she said something stupid about me trying to punish myself, and I got another D in English. I'll be lucky if I don't have to do this year over again. Not that it matters, not that any of it matters.

So where was I? Oh yeah. At Leah's house. When the police took me over to Leah's, her mother opened the door. She was holding onto the doorknob like she might fall over if she let go, and she looked a million times worse than Mom was looking. Her eyes were almost swollen shut from crying so much and when she shuffled backward to let us in, she moved like an old lady. I tried not to stare, but I couldn't believe a person could change so fast. Her voice trembled when she spoke.

"Thanks for coming over, Max. Maybe you can help the police figure out the computer better than I can. I just, I just can't understand that thing," she said, then she crumpled into a fit and Leah's dad had to pick her up off the floor.

The house was really hot and stuffy, and I thought I was going to puke. I didn't say anything, but I made my way to Leah's room. It looked like it always did – messy – and it smelled just like the vanilla Body Shop spray she always used. Her school bag was still on her floor and the clothes she'd worn to the drive-in were still in a heap in the closet.

The police officer motioned for me to sit down at the computer and I did. I logged on to her PC using the same password from back when we were both hottietoo. Luckily she had her new Hotmail name and password saved so I could sign-in automatically, because I had no idea she'd chosen "Honeybunch" as her new online name.

"You said she was talking regularly to someone online?" one of the police officers said. He stood right behind me and held onto the back of the chair, which made me feel claustrophobic.

"Yeah, she used to write to muscleboy a lot," I said as Hotmail came up on the screen.

"How did you say she met muscleboy?"

"On a music forum, the same way we met 2funE."

"Do you know his real name?"

I shook my head and suddenly it struck me that I didn't even know 2funE's real name or what he looked like or where he lived. I had imagined all these things for so long, I just assumed I knew him.

Leah's Hotmail account was filled almost to capacity. There were hundreds of messages, all of them already opened, all from muscleboy.

I opened the most recent messages, and the police and I started to read them together. Leah's mother hovered in the room and sobbed, but her father sat on the bed as still as one of Leah's stuffed animals.

I will never ever forget what that first e-mail said. I read it so many times it is etched forever in my memory.

> Hey Leah GF. I can't tell you how excited I am about seeing you. FINALLY. I can't beleive we found a way to get together. Like I always say, where there is a will there is a way. Carpe diem, seize the day. And what a day we are going to have! I hope you don't get grounded when you get back home because I know I'm going to be in the deepest crap ever for disapearing like this and for taking the old man's car. But anything is worth getting to be with you, even if it's only for one night. I'll see you at the corner where you said you'll be on Saturday morning. I'll be gone before my parents even wake up and start the coffee maker. ILYWAMH. Muscleboy.

I looked up at the police officers in shock. I didn't know whether to be angry or afraid, but my stomach dropped to the floor.

"Muscleboy sounds a lot like 2funE," I blurted out.

That's when I started to feel sick. I was exactly like Tally Hanen's little cousin, Chloe, who just happened to be playing closer to the house.

December 6

Dear Jo,

This weekend is the Port Hope Winter Fair, so Dad and Mom took us to the arena after dinner. I begged them to let me stay home, but they insisted, and I knew they weren't willing to let me stay on my own. Then I begged them to let us all stay home and not go out in the first place, but they said it would do us good, especially Molly and Gus who hadn't been outside for two days because of the rain. So I went to the stupid Winter Fair with them.

There was all the regular Winter Fair stuff like a dog show, a pet contest, a Christmas Tree display, a Christmas craft area where you could decorate miniature trees and gingerbread cookies, games, and a chance to get your picture taken sitting on Santa's lap. It wasn't bad, for a small-town thing. Molly and Gus really liked it at least. Gus especially liked the rabbits in the pet contest because they reminded him of the ones from *Teletubbies*. I felt sorry for all the animals who were being stared at by so many people and the ones who were being mauled by a hundred little kids at a time, so I said I wanted to go to the bathroom, and Dad volunteered to walk with me. Mom took Molly and Gus to the jumping castle to wear them out.

When Dad and I got back, we went to the games area. Molly and Gus played a fishing game and won little stuffed elves and I tried to win a SpongeBob SquarePants pillow by throwing darts at balloons. But I had lousy aim and missed every time. Then Dad tried and he lost too, so we didn't get one, even though I really wanted one to put on my bed. Before we left, we each got a bag of cotton candy. I ate mine while we waited for Molly and Gus to go meet Santa. There were so many people crowding around that I felt dizzy. Then at the last minute Molly said she didn't want to sit on Santa's knee. She said she wanted to go home because she felt sick to her stomach. I think it was the cotton candy that made her sick, but I didn't say anything, I just wanted to go too. Anyhow, we left and Gus missed his chance to meet Santa, but he didn't seem to mind.

There were lots of people at the fair. I saw some kids from school. I saw Emma's brother, Eric, with a group of his high school friends, but he pretended not to see me. Ever since Leah went missing, I've become invisible. Except to Lexi and Emma and Kelsey and Amanda, who swear they will never stop being my friends, ever. They say it's not my fault and

I shouldn't blame myself, but I can't help feeling responsible. I should have known something was up. I mean, Leah is my best friend and I know everything about her. Well, almost everything. But something should have triggered me. She was being so secretive and then there was that smile. It still gives me the chills. Of course, not as big as the chill I get when I remember reading muscleboy's e-mails. I will never forget that feeling of dread as it invaded my body. I just knew by the way he wrote that he was the same person as 2funE and that both Leah and I had been fooled by him, but her more than me.

By the time the police and I had gone through all of Leah's e-mails from muscleboy, we had a good idea of what had happened. Leah had gone to meet muscleboy at the corner by the high school and the Catholic church. She must have picked the high school so she would seem older, and the church on Saturday because they were having a jumble sale and there would be a lot of cars coming and going and nobody would notice her. They had been planning it for two weeks. Once she admitted to him that she didn't live in the city, he offered to come and get her. Then they were going to go back to the city for a party and then crash at his friend's house for the night. He promised to have her home by Sunday at dinner. At first I thought it was a good sign. I assumed that since she knew how much trouble she would be in when she got home, she decided to stay until Monday and have fun for one more night. But then the police looked more concerned than ever, and her parents looked as if they had stopped breathing.

After the police had read all of muscleboy's e-mails, I logged on as hottietoo and showed them the e-mails I got from 2funE. Then they packed up Leah's computer to take with them, and we got back in the car. When they dropped me back at home, Mom pulled me into her arms and gave me a big hug, even though it was the last thing I wanted. Then she looked up at the police officers as if they were the bad guys.

"I hope you didn't put her through too much."

"No, I don't think so. Thanks for letting us take her to Leah's. She was a big help."

"I hope you have a lead now."

"I hope so too. Can we call if we need to ask anything else?" The police officer was looking at me now.

"I guess. I mean, yes. I'll do anything it takes.

Just find her," I said. I was too scared to cry.

Before they left, the police took a minute to explain everything to Mom and Dad. They talked about how they suspected muscleboy and 2funE were the same person, probably a grown man, and how he had convinced Leah to go with him to the city. They said they would try to trace his accounts back to a known name and address and try to find Leah that way, that they would be in touch when they knew something more. Even after the police left, Mom and Dad never said a single word to me about how I didn't respect their decisions by going behind their backs to use the internet. I guess they sensed that I had enough to worry about.

Over the next few days the search parties combed every inch of Port Hope, and the police interviewed everyone who went to the Catholic church that morning. There were over 200 people in all, but nobody could remember seeing Leah get into a car with anyone. Emma, her parents, and I were the very last people to see Leah. Her own parents didn't even see her Saturday morning. They just found a note saying she was going to the soccer game with Emma and would be home after lunch. And it wasn't unusual for her to do that, so they didn't start to worry until she didn't show up for dinner.

Her mother went through all of her clothes to figure out what she was wearing, just so the police could put out a description of what she looked like. Officially, Leah was wearing denim capris, a navy tank top and a grey Gap hoodie. She had on tan sandals, and her hair was probably in a ponytail.

Each night when I got home from school that week, Mom dragged me into her arms as soon as I walked in the door. She kept looking at me with this funny, thankful look. I wanted to make her feel better whenever I found her crying, so I'd tell her I loved her and that I was safe and so were Molly and Gus, but then she'd start crying harder and that made me feel worse.

December 7

Dear Jo,

Within two days of her disappearance, Leah's picture was on the local news and has been all over the newspapers and on flyers ever since. It's even on missing kids' Web sites all over the world. No matter where I look, her face is there, smiling at me: from the TV, from telephone poles, at McDonald's and

Wal-Mart. Each time I see her, I think how pretty she is with her long honey hair and brown eyes, and I miss her so much I have to sit down. It was her grade six school picture that they used. In it she was wearing a jean jacket and had two butterfly clips in her hair. I remember her finally picking that outfit, after trying on three others while I waited to walk to school with her. I told her it wouldn't matter what she picked. She looked good in everything.

For the first few weeks I couldn't believe she was missing. It was like my brain refused to cooperate, even though I fed it all the right information. I couldn't, I can't, believe she was taken in the middle of the day without anyone seeing anything. Surely she would have screamed and kicked when a grown man tried to drag her into his car. Surely she knew enough to make a big scene. But if she did, there are no witnesses. It makes no sense.

I don't think anyone else can believe it either. I remember going downstairs to say goodnight to Mom and Dad that first night and seeing Leah's parents on the news. Her mother couldn't even speak she was crying so hard, but her father asked whoever had her to please bring her home safe. Her aunt and uncle were on the TV too, looking upset and standing under Leah's parents' arms to hold them up. When Mom saw me watching from behind the couch she changed the channel.

At first I couldn't sleep at night. I'd lie in my bed and wonder where Leah was and think about how scared she must be. I would picture her in a run-down cabin in the woods or in a basement or an attic or in the trunk of a car. I would try to fall asleep, but I couldn't. I would wonder if she was cold or hungry or hurt. Every time I closed my eyes, I'd see some big man trying to take Leah and shove her in his car. Or I'd see him trying to grab me or Molly. Then I'd turn on the light by my bed and try to go to sleep again. But it never seemed to work and would disturb Molly. So I started turning on Molly's nightlight and crawling into bed with her to feel safe. The first few nights I wanted to get Gus too, so that he wouldn't be alone, but I knew if I moved him he would wake up and Mom would be upset. That's about the time Mom started feeding me those little white sleeping pills. She got them from our family doctor because she said I wasn't sleeping at all, that I was like a zombie during the day because I was so exhausted. She was afraid I would snap if I didn't get some sleep. So the doctor gave us some low-dose sleeping pills. Mom only gave them to me on the worst nights, then I would fall into a dark, motionless sleep without dreams.

December 8

Dear Jo,

The week Leah went missing we had an assembly in the gym and the police came to talk about stranger dangers. All the girls were serious and paying attention, but when we got back to class I heard some of the boys making a joke about it. I was so mad I started yelling at them, and Mrs. Evans had to take me out to the hall to calm me down. The boys said nobody else would ever get taken in Port Hope again because all the girls left were too ugly. When I told Mrs. Evans this, she looked ready to explode. Everyone stopped talking when we came back into the classroom, and it was so quiet, it was eerie. She stared long and hard at those boys for a minute, then told them off in a slow, stern way. They looked sorry when she was done. Then we reviewed the stranger danger tips we'd talked about in assembly.

When I got home from school, I told Mom about our assembly and about what we learned.

She looked relieved. We discussed a family code word and came up with one that we can use in case of an emergency – in case Mom or Dad has to send someone we don't know to pick us up and we need to know that they are to be trusted. Mom made me swear to keep the word to myself, not to tell anyone, not even Lexi or Emma or Kelsey or Amanda. I can't even write it down here because it's so completely top secret. We haven't even told Molly yet, because she can't keep a secret very well and is likely to blab it during "show-and-tell" or something.

December 10

Dear Jo,

That June, it was hard to concentrate on year-end tests when Leah was still missing and her desk sat empty at the front of the room. I barely passed grade six and only squeaked by based on the marks I got at the beginning of the year. How could I care about math or reading when my best friend was gone? I couldn't help but wonder if Leah realized she was missing her year-end tests. I couldn't help but wonder if she could see or hear the news wherever she was. I couldn't help but wonder if she had any idea that so many people were looking for her.

All the neighbors helped to search for her, and the search went on for twelve weeks straight. I even took time off school to join in, then used some of my summer vacation to make lemonade and sandwiches for the men who were searching in the bush and hills outside of town. Mom was against me searching, but I insisted. To start, we went through all the parks and neighborhoods and the school yards to look for evidence. We walked shoulder to shoulder for miles and miles, turning over every blade of grass. But by the end of the first week, there was still no evidence and no leads. The police also went door to door through Leah's neighborhood to interview people. They logged a thousand hours of interviews and still had nothing.

It's been more then six months now, and the search parties have stopped, but I think about finding her every day or of seeing or remembering some clue that will help the police find her. It's not such a crazy thought. I mean, Elizabeth Smart was gone for nine months and she came home safe and sound. I heard that Elizabeth's little sister remembered a clue seven months after Elizabeth disappeared and that led the police to identify and catch the man, to find Elizabeth. And every five or six weeks the police make another public appeal and air the details of Leah's disappearance, just to help trigger a memory in someone. They even had Leah's case on *America's Most Wanted* not long after she went missing. Someone, somewhere, somehow has to remember something. There just has to be a break in this case soon.

December 12

Dear Jo,

Dad came up to talk to me tonight about getting my own room. He still didn't say "No," but he asked me to wait until spring before we talk about it again. He said it's too cold down there right now and that they want to keep a closer eye on me for the time being. But he stressed – he even said so – that he wasn't saying absolutely no. Of course, it feels that way.

December 14

Dear Jo,

Last night there was a candlelight vigil for Leah in Lost Lake Park. Mom went out in the afternoon and bought some really big candles and a lighter. She said the store was almost completely out of candles and she got the last of the pillar kind. After dinner we got ready to go. Dad stayed home with Molly and Gus because they're too young to be out in the cold at night, but he gave me a big hug before we left and told me to light a candle for him too. Emma and Lexi came in our car, and Kelsey and Amanda followed in Kelsey's mother's car.

There were so many people in town that there was a traffic jam at the main lights and people were streaming down the sidewalks. Every parking lot in town was full, so we had to find a place on the street. Then we had to walk for a long way. I'd never been in such a big crowd in Port Hope before, all heading in the same direction, everyone carrying blankets and candles and shuffling sadly along. But Mom stayed close by me and I felt pretty safe. I think there were people from all over, not just from Port Hope.

It was an amazing sight. The park was filled with thousands of people and thousands of candles, and the night was alive with flickering lights. It was freezing out, which was okay while we were walking, but once we stood still, I got cold. I couldn't stop shivering, so Mom put a sleeping bag around me and cuddled me. Then we huddled together in the dark in that huge crowd and watched the candles burning and burning. The whole park looked like it was filled with twinkling stars. There was a group of people singing hymns like *Amazing Grace*, but other than that, there was only the sound of shuffling bodies and sniffling noses.

At first I didn't think I had any tears left in me, that I was cried out from all the crying I did during the summer, but then I couldn't help myself, the tears just came, and kept coming, even when I tried to stop. There were a lot of people crying loudly, especially Lexi and Emma and me. We could have made a river with all the tears people were shedding. It was a good thing Mom had a bunch of tissues because everyone needed them.

We cried as we filed past a huge collage pegged in the ground. At the top it said, "We love you, Leah," and under the words were pictures of Leah from the time she was a baby until just before she went missing. We had to wait in a long line to see the pictures, but I'm glad we did. There was a picture of all of us last year when we went horseback riding at Kelsey's and another of us at Amanda's sleepover in grade five. There was a picture of her and her mother cuddling on a hammock and a picture of her and her father with wet hair in a swimming pool. I especially liked the picture of her sitting on a bench at the baseball park, smiling out from under her cap. Under the collage there was a heap of flowers, notes, cards, and teddy bears. We looked all around for her parents, but they weren't anywhere to be seen.

We stayed for a couple of hours and then decided it was time to go home because we were shivering through our blankets. A lot of people were leaving, but the park was still full of people huddled together beside their candles. We left our candles burning and walked to the car. I looked back when we'd walked a few feet away, but couldn't make out our candles from the rest.

December 16

Dear Jo,

Only four more days until Amanda's Christmas sleepover. Every year during the holidays, Amanda has Lexi, Kelsey, Emma, me, and Leah over for a pajama party. We've been doing it since kinder-garten. I wasn't sure we would still have it this year, but I guess our parents talked about it and thought it would be good for us. I think they mostly thought it would be good for me. I'm not even sure I want to go. I mean, it won't be the same without Leah, and everyone will expect me to talk and be happy. And I'm just not up for it. I used to look forward to the sleepover for weeks. In grade three I marked it on the calendar two months ahead of time and asked every morning how many more sleeps. It drove Mom crazy. But I'm dreading it this year ...

Amanda just called to tell me what movies she got. Maybe it won't be so bad if we watch movies all night. Then at least I won't have to make small talk. Because how can I find the energy to talk when all I do is think about Leah every minute of every day?

After *America's Most Wanted* aired last June, the police started getting tips about Leah's case, but not from people in Port Hope. Somehow muscleboy swooped into town without being seen. It was almost as if he had an invisibility cloak, like in Harry Potter. There wasn't one eyewitness who saw an unfamiliar car or face in Port Hope that Saturday. But once the news of Leah spread, the public started to phone in tips and before long they realized muscleboy had been writing to about twenty young girls using different online identities and pretending to be a young boy.

I can't help but wonder what would have happened if I had agreed to meet 2funE. I know I'd be the one missing, not Leah. Then she would be the one searching in ditches and playgrounds. Sometimes I imagine Mom and Dad and Molly and Gus crying all the time and trying to talk on the news. I can barely stand to think about it, but I can't help myself either.

One night I overheard Mom and Dad talking in their room. I shouldn't have been listening in on their private conversation, but I couldn't help myself when I heard Leah's name. Dad said, "I don't think they are going to find her alive." I imagined that Mom shot him a shriveling look because she said, "All the more reason to pray for her and her family."

I still pray for her every night, sometimes for hours, but nothing good ever comes of it. I'm not sure whether or not to believe in God anymore.

December 17

Dear Jo,

Shortly after Leah's story aired on *America's Most Wanted*, Detective Lucas came to our house to talk to Mom and Dad and me. He wasn't dressed like a cop or anything, because he works undercover. And he wasn't driving a police car, just a blue Ford. He told us the police weren't able to trace muscleboy or 2funE through his e-mail accounts and were no closer to finding him than they had been the day they took me to help them log on to Leah's computer. They were pretty sure they were dealing with a computer expert, someone who could hack the systems and hide his trail. But they also thought *I* could help catch Leah's killer. He wanted me to start writing to 2funE again, to try luring *him* into meeting with *me* so the police could catch him red-handed. With all of the e-mails 2funE wrote to Leah and me and all those other girls who came forward, they'd put together a psychological profile on him. But they said, next to Leah, he was closest with me. They hoped there would be something I could say to get him interested again, just in e-mailing to start. I didn't know whether to be excited or scared. I mean, I wanted to help them get this creep, but I wasn't sure I could face writing to him again. And they were sure he was going to be more wary, since there was so much publicity about Leah's disappearance and because of the fact she was lured away by an internet predator.

Mom was so against it from the very beginning, but Dad made her listen to the detective. At the time, I didn't say much because I was too scared and confused. Detective Lucas didn't stay long that first visit. He suggested we take a day or two to talk about it. But by the time he finished talking, I was convinced that he needed my help, and I couldn't imagine not doing it. I just wanted to bring Leah back and get that creep off the streets.

Detective Lucas was really cool. He wasn't as old as Dad and was way more in tune with things my friends and I like. He knew all about MySpace, instant messaging, and the best places to download MP3s. I know all of this because we had a chat before he left, while Dad and Mom were in the living room *discussing* things. Detective Lucas told me I could make a difference and that he would never put me in danger. He told me I would be safe and that I could always trust him. He had really nice brown eyes. I felt like he sort of understood me or something.

After Molly and Gus went to bed, Mom and Dad and I spent a long time talking about what to do. Of course Mom said no.

She said, "Surely he can find someone else. I

mean, Maxine has been so stressed lately. She's been through so much. I don't think this is the best thing for her. Besides, how can we trust our daughter to some stranger, even if he is a police officer?"

"Mom, I'm sitting right here," I said. I hate when she talks about me as if I'm in another room.

"I'm sorry, sweetie, but I just don't like this idea. As much as I want Leah back, as much as I want this guy in jail, I don't want to take the risk. I can't. I refuse to let you get involved."

"Debbie, think about this rationally. Detective Lucas said they'd given it a lot of thought and Maxine is their best shot. This guy is going to know how Maxine writes and thinks, what she says and how she says it. He's an expert at getting into kids' minds and, as upsetting as it is, he's been into Maxine's head. He'll recognize a fake in a second, and then the opportunity would be lost forever. This may be the only way to find Leah. Wouldn't you want Leah to help if the situation was reversed?"

"I know, but ..." was Mom's reply.

"They wouldn't consider getting her involved if they didn't need her. Besides, you heard what he said. She'll be safe. She'll be protected and supervised by the police at every step."

"I just don't know."

"Maxine, what do you think? It should be your decision."

At least Dad didn't treat me like a two-year-old. I thought for a minute before saying anything, and as I started to speak, it became clear.

"Maybe I should. I mean, I'm not going to be at any risk writing e-mails. 2funE still doesn't know who I am. If it's going to help us find Leah, how can I say no? Maybe it will help me feel better if I do this. And maybe I can save someone else from disappearing."

"Listen to her, Debbie. She's making a lot of sense. She's bright and mature and I think she can do this. We'll keep a close watch on everything," Dad said.

Dad walked over and sat down on the couch between Mom and me. He put an arm around both of us and squeezed. Mom didn't speak for a long time, and we just sat and listened to the furnace pumping hot air into the room.

"Okay," Mom conceded. "But just you know that I'll put a stop to it if things go too far." Her voice was trembling, and she stood up after that and left.

So that was that. Dad called Detective Lucas and said I'd do it. Then I talked to Detective Lucas on the phone and he was really glad. He said, "Welcome to the team, Max. I think you're going to be terrific."

I liked the way he called me Max, the way my friends do.

The next day I went to the police station to write my first e-mail. I knew exactly what to say:

> Hey 2funE BF. Sorry I've been off-line for a few weeks. First we were on vacation and since then things have been unbearable at home because I broke my curfew again and got grounded, so I couldn't use my computer. Parents! You'd think I was a five-year-old the way they treat me. You know? Anyhow, my mom finally decided I was responsible enough to use the internet again... I hope you weren't sad when you didn't hear from me for so long. I felt soooo bad that I couldn't write back. Believe me, I would have if I could have. I hope you understand. I've had to work really hard to

get her trust. I've been babysitting and cleaning the house non-stop. I feel like Cinderella. I've missed you so much it's driving me crazy. How 'bout you? Or have you found another QT to write to? TOY.

After that e-mail, I just *knew* we were going to catch the guy and rescue Leah. I was anxious for days, waiting for it all to be over and imagining how great it was going to be when I saw her finally. I so badly wanted to bring her home. We waited and waited and watched and watched. After two weeks I called Detective Lucas to see if I should try again and he said yes. So I did.

> Hey 2funE BF. My heart is breaking. Not just because you won't write back, but because I let you down. Even if you ever do forgive me, I may not forgive myself. I won't forget you and I'll keep waiting, 4-ever. Your online QT. Hottietoo.

When I hit send I hoped with all my heart I'd written the right thing to entice 2funE back online. I knew it was the best that I could come up with, and Detective Lucas said it was perfect because it left an open invitation. So we began waiting again. I called Detective Lucas three times a day for a week to have him check my Hotmail account and give me any updates. But that wasn't necessary. He was watching it already. In the end, 2funE never did write back, at least he hasn't yet, and it's been six months. I feel like it's one more thing I've failed. I feel awful for letting Detective Lucas down and especially for letting Leah down again. I still wonder if I should have written something different, even though Detective Lucas has told me about twenty times that it isn't my fault, that 2funE is probably just too scared to write back. He tells me to call if I remember anything important. And every time we talk he tells me not to worry, that they'll find another way to find Leah, and that they have a whole team on the case.

December 18

Dear Jo,

We put up our Christmas tree tonight. Dad and Molly went to town to buy it while Mom made hot chocolate and I played with Gus. It's a pretty nice tree, and Molly is excited about it, but I'm having a hard time being cheerful, even for her sake. Mom gave me spending money to buy some presents, even though I have my babysitting money.

She said, "At least get something for Molly and Gus. Oh, and Granny." She also asked me again what I wanted, but I couldn't think of anything, except Leah, which I knew I shouldn't say. So I just let my eyes fill up with tears and said it didn't matter.

Leah has been gone for almost seven months now, 211 days to be exact. In the beginning I was sure it was a matter of time until she came back. But now I just don't know what to think. I'm afraid to think about it.

December 19

Dear Jo,

America's Most Wanted aired Leah's segment again last week, and now a big story has hit the news! I saw it on TV after dinner. In March, right around the time Leah and I were always on Habbo Hotel, a girl sneaked off to her local McDonald's without her parents' permission. She went to meet someone she knew as Sk8er8, and he tried to get her into his car. They aren't releasing her name, but the girl told police she had gone to meet a boy, and when she got there, a man met her instead, saying he was Sk8er8's father. He claimed his son had just broken his arm and was resting at home, but that he would drive the girl over so she could still meet his son as planned. The girl said it was okay and she would arrange to meet Sk8er8 another time, that she wasn't allowed to get into a stranger's car. She said she didn't come forward sooner because she was afraid her parents would be angry if they found out what she'd done. She was only ten at the time.

So now the police have a description of the car and a drawing of the man and both were on the news tonight. He is extremely creepy looking – he has a skinny face and short stubbly hair, which the police say is now probably longer. They also suggested he could have grown a beard.

I stared and stared at the picture in the newspaper. I couldn't believe that it was probably my 2funE.

December 20

Dear Jo,

I'm at Amanda's for the sleepover, and it is just after 3:00 in the morning. Everyone else is asleep, but I'm still awake. I'm glad I came. After the movies, we painted our nails crazy colors then listened to Sum 41 until Amanda's mother told us to turn off the music. We didn't talk about Leah much, but we made her Christmas cards and wrote her special notes, and I volunteered to drop them off at her house tomorrow to add to everything else that is there.

Ever since she disappeared, the whole front of Leah's house has been covered in flowers and cards and candles, hundreds of them burning so the air smells of hot wax all the time. When Mom first saw it, she said it was a better shrine than the one for Princess Di in England. Whenever I go by, I can't believe the mountain of flowers that are there. Fresh ones every day. People drive from the city to sit and look at the stuff piled there or to read the notes and cards. There are even stuffed bears. In the early days, I left my original blue Sherbert The Bear in the pile because Leah always wanted one. After that Mom bought me a replacement. The police were there every day too, at first, watching to see if anyone suspicious showed up. And there is a huge picture of Leah someone put up, the same one that was in the newspaper and on the TV and a big sign saying, "We're going to bring you home, Leah." It's so hopeful and sad at the same time.

December 21

Dear Jo,

Granny arrived today full of "twitters and smiles," as Dad says. He also said she looks a lot older than she did in the summer, but Mom said she looks the same and is still full of "vim and vinegar." Sometimes I don't get adult sayings. Whatever it means, the first thing Granny did was insist on taking us kids uptown and buying us all treats. So we got bundled up and loaded Gus into the stroller. Molly perched on the front, and we started walking. Granny said how pretty the houses looked with all the Christmas lights and how much she missed Port Hope, how she yearned for it, and if she had the courage, she would move back now that Granddad is dead.

"This place reminds me of being your age," she said with that sentimental way old people have of talking, the way that means you're supposed to ask a question so they can keep remembering out loud to you.

"You lived here when you were my age?" I said, even though I didn't want to think about her being twelve at all.

"Yes, I did."

"Are you pretty old now?" Molly asked, and Granny laughed.

"I guess so, but I've still got a few good years left."

"Left for what?" Molly asked.

"Left for living," Granny said.

"Before you start loosing your teeth and hair?"

"Molly, dear," Granny said. "I lost all my teeth years ago."

Then she popped out her teeth and dropped them in her hand. They're dentures and she leaves them in a glass of water at night. It's really gross. I guess Granny thought Molly would think it was cool to pop out your teeth, but Molly started screaming. With Molly screaming, Gus joined in.

"Molly thinks that once you start losing your teeth, you fall apart and then float up to heaven," I tried to explain over the racket.

"Where on earth would she get an idea like that?" Granny asked.

I just shrugged and said, "I dunno."

When she calmed down enough, Molly pulled out her tooth necklace and showed Granny. Between sniffles she said, "See, it's already started happening to me and I'm only little."

That made Granny laugh again. By that time we were on the main street, and people were staring at Granny laughing, Molly crying, and Gus screaming just to hear his own voice. We must have looked like a bunch of lunatics. I wanted to become a ghost and disappear before I saw someone from school.

When we got home I stayed in the living room and watched *Arthur* on TV with Molly and Gus. I'm afraid to be alone with Granny because I know she'll want to talk about Leah, the way she did in the summer when she was here. Keeping close to Molly must work though, or else Mom told her not to mention it, because she hasn't tried to corner me yet.

December 22

Dear Jo,

Mom took Molly and me Christmas shopping. Talk about leaving it to the last minute. Normally we have our shopping done by the middle of December, but this is not a normal year. We left Gus with Granny because he always runs away in big stores and we were going to Wal-Mart. Molly was very excited to be coming, especially when Gus was being left behind. I bought Molly a new Polly

Pocket set and Gus a Bob-the-Builder tractor. I got Granny two cinnamon-scented candles and still had enough left over to buy Mom some jasmine bath salts and Dad an Eagles CD that was in the reduced bin. He loves that oldies music. I ran out of money for Aunt Laurie, but Mom said she had a set of Christmas tea towels I could give her.

On the way home from shopping, I asked Mom to drive by Leah's house so I could drop off the Christmas cards we'd made at Amanda's sleepover. There weren't many candles burning and a lot of the flowers were covered over because it's been snowing today, but there were still some Christmas cards and wreaths and even a plate of cookies. Her mom must have taken all the teddy bears inside to keep them dry. Mom parked the car and I ran up the driveway to leave the cards on top of the pile. It felt very lonely. I guess people are losing hope. I feel myself losing a little bit of hope every day, even though I don't do it on purpose. It drips out of me. I try to stop it in case it's the hope that's going to bring her home, but there's nothing I can do to keep it in.

I used to think I could feel her out there, that I could feel her thinking of me, and I'd try really hard to use some type of psychic power and communicate with her. But now I wonder if it was just wishful thinking, because the signal's gotten really weak. I can't tell what I feel anymore. I can't separate what I feel from what I want to feel. It's all jumbled up inside, and the more I try to figure it out, the more I get confused.

December 23

Dear Jo,

Detective Lucas called our house tonight. My heart soared when Mom handed me the phone and said who was calling. I thought for sure I was getting an early Christmas present, that the most recent AMW segment had brought in a solid lead. But there was no good news. He just called to tell us he would continue working, even over the holidays. He said there'd been a few more girls who had come forward about boys who wanted to meet in person after having met online, but they weren't connected to muscleboy or 2funE.

Before he said goodbye, he asked again if there was anything else I'd remembered, but I had to tell him no. I promised again to call if I thought of anything, and he promised to call if he learned anything. I guess he could hear the discouragement in my voice because he told me not to get down.

"A case like this could break at any time, Max. It only takes the slightest lead, what seems like the most insignificant detail, to put us on the right track. I haven't given up yet and neither should you. Just try and enjoy Christmas and don't think about things too much. You might remember something if you give your mind a break."

So now of course, I'm trying not to think too hard in case I'm keeping an important clue locked in my mind. Then I notice I'm thinking too hard about trying not to think too hard and all I end up with is a big fat headache.

December 24

Dear Jo,

Tomorrow is Christmas and we are ready at last, even though I can tell nobody's heart is really into it. Aunt Laurie came up for a few days, like she always does. She asked me if I was writing in my "diary," and I said, "Yes." I didn't bother to tell her you are a *journal*.

Tonight after dinner we bundled up and went outside for a walk to look at all the houses decorated and lit up with Christmas lights. We pulled Molly and Gus in the toboggan and shared a thermos of hot chocolate as we walked. The whole Christmas-Eve-walk-thing is a tradition in our family that I guess dates back to when Grandma was my age. We go every year, even if there's a blizzard. Tonight it was snowing – the big, exaggerated, fluffy flakes that look like they belong on a postcard or in a movie – so the lawns and trees and houses were covered in a delicate duvet of lace. It was a beautiful evening and everyone pretended to be happy. But the act was only for Molly and Gus.

I walked most of the way with the adults, but then Gus wanted "Zine on bogan," and Dad said he was sure he could pull all three of his kids for a little way. So I got on the toboggan behind Gus and Molly and rode the rest of the way home with them cuddled up against me. At first Dad pretended I was too heavy to pull and made everyone laugh when he grunted and strained to make the toboggan move, but I don't really think my weight made that much of a difference because Dad is pretty strong. The adults walked ahead and commented on how pretty the houses looked and, even though I wasn't part of their adult conversation, I could hear everything they said. I preferred being warm and close to Molly and Gus where we didn't have to talk.

When we came back inside we got ready for bed, and Granny read us *The Night Before Christmas*, like she does every year. Then we put out a plate of cookies and a glass of milk for Santa and a carrot for Rudolph. Molly asked why we didn't leave carrots for all of the reindeer, but Mom said, "Don't worry. Other people leave carrots too, so there will be plenty to go around." Right now Molly and Gus are tucked into bed. Molly is sound asleep on her back, snoring just a little and, as usual, I'm under my covers writing to you. The adults are downstairs stuffing the stockings, and I can just barely hear their voices drifting up the stairs. Otherwise the house is very quiet.

I'm trying not to imagine what it's like at Leah's house tonight or where Leah is on Christmas Eve. Instead, I'm trying to relax my mind so that any important clues can get out. Of course, it's impossible to clear my head with so many thoughts swirling around. It's just one more way I'm letting Leah down. See, there I go again, putting too much pressure on myself, getting anxious and blaming myself the way everyone tells me I shouldn't.

December 25

Merry Christmas, Leah. Wherever you are. Emma gave me a framed picture of all of us from that summer when we went out to Loon Lake to go swimming. Remember that? How we tanned on the rocks all afternoon and jumped off the cliffs? You looked really happy. You have no idea how much it hurts to have you gone.

I wonder if Detective Lucas has taken a day off from looking for you? I hope not. If I didn't know that every square inch of Port Hope has already been searched, I'd go out looking for you myself.

December 28

Dear Jo,

It finally happened! Ever since last June I've been having the same haunting dream about Leah, and it always leaves me feeling hollow inside. In my dream, Leah is huddled in a corner of an empty house, shivering from the cold. When I walk in, she is happy to see me and I give her my coat. I tell her I'm going to get her home where she belongs, and she looks really sad. She says she can't go home, that she's lost her way. So I take her to the window to look out, and all we can see is white, like there is a really thick fog outside. But last night I dreamed we actually stepped outside the house and into all that white. We still couldn't see a thing, but I could feel a fence with my hands, and I started to follow it. I told Leah to hold on to my back and I made my way along the fence. Then I couldn't feel her following me anymore, and I stopped to wait for her. I called her name, but she never answered. I waited and waited and called and called, until my voice gave out. Then the fog cleared and I saw I was standing in a farmer's field all alone. That's when I woke up. I was shivering because my comforter had fallen on the floor. I wonder if this is a sign? I'll have to call Detective Lucas to tell him.

December 29

Dear Jo,

I called Detective Lucas about my dream. He thought it was good news, that I was giving myself permission to think and feel and remember again. But the really good news is that they think they have a lead! A fourteen-year-old girl was solicited while she was in a Tomb Raider chatroom. A "fifteen-year-old boy" tried to convince her to meet him so that they could go play laser tag together. He said it was time to "seize the day" and make the most of her school holidays. I'm not allowed to tell anyone, but the detectives are trying to trace the user back to an e-mail account and address right now.

January 1

Happy New Year, Leah. It's been an awful year. I'm glad it's over. You must know that my New Year's wish is to bring you home.

January 5

Dear Jo,

I survived the first day back at school after the break. It was as awful as I thought it would be, but at least it's over. Our grade seven teacher, Mr. Conroy, asked us to write a story or poem that he's going to submit to a writing contest. Poems can be any format. Stories can be about anything, but they have to be fiction and have to have dialogue. Our first draft is due in one week. The problem is, I don't feel like writing a story or a poem. I don't even feel like thinking. Why doesn't he understand that it's hard to care about writing a story or poem when you've lost your best friend? I don't even know how the others can care enough to pretend to care. They seem to have forgotten about Leah and it makes me really angry. They still talk at recess about what happened on *Survivor* or *American Idol* or what Malcolm did to Reese, as if those things are real and important. They even think this writing assignment is exciting. Lexi is already plotting her story. But I just don't care about any of it.

I guess part of the problem is that I don't like Mr. Conroy and haven't since I got in his class in September. I know he's trying really hard, but it bugs me the way he acts so happy all the time, as if he doesn't even know Leah is missing. The only good thing about him is that he doesn't play favorites – it's driving Gracie mad because last year, Mrs. Evans always asked Gracie to take the attendance sheet down to the office, which made her gloat. No wonder she hardly has any friends.

I had my first session of the year with my therapist today. When she asked what I've been doing, I told her I was writing in a journal almost every day and that seemed to make her happy. Adults are obsessed with me writing in a journal. They look so relieved when I tell them I've been scribbling away. I wish it would make me that happy. I didn't tell her about the dream I had. I didn't want to have to talk and think about it and risk clogging the airways. Ever since I had that dream, I feel like something important is finally trying to get through.

January 6

Dear Jo,

There was a piece on the news tonight about a high school girl who was contacted through her personal Web page to pose for pictures at a photography studio in the city. The photographer had seen her picture on MySpace, thought she had what it takes to be a model, and offered to take some pictures for her portfolio. She didn't go to meet the man, but contacted the police instead. When they searched his studio and his computer, they found hundreds of images of naked children. Now the guy is in police custody and is being charged with possessing child pornography. Of course, the police are looking into links with other cases. Maybe he's connected to Leah ...

January 7

Dear Jo,

I missed class this morning because I had to get my braces tightened again. The orthodontist said he is pleased with how my teeth are moving into place and that I might be able to get the braces off early if I'm lucky. I won't get my hopes up.

Mom and Dad had a huge fight tonight. I know it was big because Dad took us out to dinner – even Gus – to Napoli's Pizza, and Mom didn't come. She didn't even come out of her room. Dad said she had a headache, which is never the truth. Why are adults allowed to lie?

Going out to dinner was weird because Mom wasn't there and Dad was sad and quiet. I told Dad I'd rather stay home to take care of Mom and maybe just heat up some tomato soup, but he insisted I come along. Molly insisted that her imaginary friend, Georgia, come along too. We had to leave room for her to sit in the car and we had to leave the door to the restaurant open long enough so she could get in. Then we had to sit at a table with an empty seat and a glass of water because Molly said Georgia needed something to drink, and Dad wouldn't buy her a chocolate milk. I felt like an idiot including Georgia in our conversation, but Dad needed the distraction and it kept Molly happy. Gus was pretty good, better than he usually is in restaurants, and sat the whole time in the high chair eating breadsticks and drinking chocolate milk from his sippy cup. I got a personal-size Hawaiian pizza, which is usually my favorite, but tonight it just tasted like rubber. At least my teeth hadn't started to hurt yet.

When we got home, Dad went into his office to catch up on his work, and Mom came out and gave Molly and Gus baths and read them stories. Even though it's fun going out to eat, I hate it when my parents fight because the house gets really quiet and I feel bad for whoever is being left out. I like it better when we all get along. I hope they weren't fighting about me, but I'm sure they were. I'm sure it was something about my "state of mind." Mom thinks I need more help than I'm getting, and Dad thinks I just need time to work it out myself. I'm with Dad.

January 8

Dear Jo,

I decided to write a poem to Leah for the writing contest. Here's my first draft.

To Leah, My Best Friend

I hope you can see the world,
From wherever you are.
Our tears, our fears, our sadness,
For you, our fallen star.

You were here one minute,
But then you were gone.
And nobody understands,
Why you've been away so long.

Your family can't stop crying,
We heap flowers at your home,
We all have each other,
But you are all alone.

Everyone feels the hole,
That's left in your place.

And all we can do is stare,
At your school picture face.

January 9

Dear Jo,

Mr. Conroy asked me to stay after class today. I thought I was in trouble for something, but I didn't know what. So I sat at my desk as everyone else left the room, and Lexi looked back at me to see if I was worried. I wasn't really. What could Mr. Conroy do that could make things any worse than they already are? It turned out he just wanted to talk to me about my poem. He asked me if I wrote poems often.

"No, never," I said.

"Did you get help?" he asked.

"No," I said. "I wrote it last night before I went to sleep."

He looked surprised. "Just one draft?"

"You *said* we just had to hand in our first draft today."

"I know. That's fine. I'm just surprised you got it in one go."

"I scratched out some words, but then recopied it."

"Well, it's very good," he said.

"Thanks," I said, because what else could I really say?

"Do you mind if I submit it to a magazine, besides the contest?"

"No, I don't mind. But can I go now? I have to pick up my little sister in the kindergarten class, and she'll get upset if I'm late."

He smiled and nodded, then I ran off and found Molly almost in tears because she was the last one in the classroom with her teacher.

Also, I had some disappointing news from Detective Lucas tonight. The girl who was invited to play laser tag admits that she had a friend write the e-mail, just to get attention. I'm beyond disappointed. How could she do such a terrible thing? She acts like it's a game, but it's not. The detectives might have wasted valuable time chasing that lead, time that might have helped them get closer to finding Leah.

January 10

Dear Jo,

The parental fight seems to be over, or at least

better. We're back to eating as a family again, and Mom and Dad are talking to each other a little bit. When Mom came to tuck Molly in tonight, I told her I hoped they weren't fighting about me, and she said, "It didn't have to do with anything you should worry about." But how can I not worry about it? Parents split up all the time and it's really awful. I don't think I could stand it if my parents lived in different houses and I had to go back and forth all the time.

Kelsey's parents split up when she was in grade three and now she lives with her mom and step-dad and has to put up with a step-sister who never does her share of the chores and whines all the time. That's one of the reasons I hate going to sleepovers at Kelsey's. I can't stand her step-sister, Allie, hanging out with us. And if Kelsey complains, her mother says she has to be nice because Allie doesn't have a mom. Kelsey says Allie steals all the attention and lies to get her in trouble. But I probably shouldn't get so worked up about it all. I bet Leah would be happy just to be home, even if her parents were fighting or if they split up or lived on different planets.

January 12

Dear Jo,

I feel so sick I can't eat or sleep and I missed school today. I don't think I'll ever go back. I don't think I'll do anything ever again. I wish I could just stop breathing and die. I can't stand to think about it, and I'm not even sure I can write it.

They found Leah's body. She was in the forest east of the city. A farmer found her yesterday when he was walking his dog. The weather's been really mild this week, so all the snow melted and left her exposed. The police say she's been there for months and months, just lying there, all alone. But the leaves and undergrowth hid her in the summer and fall. She left her bones behind and went up to heaven.

I saw her family on the news tonight and they were a mess. Her mom didn't stop crying the whole time and looked like she hadn't slept in about a year. Even her aunt and uncle were crying and had puffy eyes and red faces. Her dad managed to say a few words. He said they were reliving the nightmare over again, but he thanked everyone for their support and prayers. Mom is a mess too. I'm an even bigger mess. I think I already knew Leah was dead, but knowing it for real is like going back to the beginning to when she first went missing. There are still so many unanswered questions. Whenever I close my eyes, I see her lying there cold and alone, and my throat squeezes so tight I think I'm going to choke. I know it could be me lying there dead, and in a way, I think it would be better if it was. It hurts too much to still be here.

January 15

Dear Jo,

I missed the last three days of school and today Mr. Conroy called Mom to see if I was okay. She explained that I was upset about Leah and just needed a few days to rest. She said she was taking time off work too. He asked if he could come by and see me, and she said yes. So he came after school, and we went to the living room to talk. First we just talked about the assignments I've missed and how I could make up the work. Or, at least, he talked about all of that and I just pretended to listen. I honestly don't think he cares about the schoolwork at all. He was just checking up on me. Everyone is worried about me again, I can tell.

He said, "It's not just about the schoolwork, you know. You're a big part of the class. The other kids miss you. I miss you. It's not the same when you're not there."

"Really?" I said. I didn't believe him.

"Absolutely."

"You mean besides Amanda and Kelsey and Lexi and Emma?"

"I mean everyone. All twenty-seven of us. You're very well-liked, you know. Anyhow, I came by for another reason too."

I didn't answer – just looked at him and waited for him to go on.

"I know about a publishing company that is asking for writing submissions from students to print in a book in honor of Leah. They approached me because they knew she would have been in our class, and they wanted to give her friends a chance to submit something special. Would you mind if I submitted your poem for Leah? Your name would be printed with it so everyone would know who wrote it."

I paused and thought about what he was saying.

"I guess it would be okay." I didn't feel anything

about it one way or the other.

Then he looked uncomfortable and said he hoped to see me Monday, that sometimes it's better to keep busy. As if I could find a way to distract myself from thinking about Leah being dead. The only difference now that I know she's really dead is that instead of trying to rescue her, I think more about getting the guy who killed her.

January 17

Dear Jo,

Today was Leah's funeral. It was the most awful thing. Worse than I even imagined. The church was so packed, people were standing in the yard in a snowstorm during the service, and the street was swarming with reporters and cameramen. I think most of Port Hope was there, plus there were people from other places, even the city. I think every police officer from one hundred miles away was there, and every street all the way back to our house was lined with cars. Even Detective Lucas was there, and when he had a chance after the service, he came over to assure me that he wouldn't let this guy get away. He said that even after all these months, they'd be able to find some evidence on Leah's remains that would lead them to her killer. Somehow, with all my mixed up emotions swirling around, that little bit of news was good.

Mrs. Barnes stayed with Molly and Gus, while Mom and Dad and I went to the funeral. We went to the church early to get a seat, and it was already packed. We were lucky to be able to sit in a pew reserved for family and friends. I couldn't hear a word the minister said because the crying was so loud. Dad said Leah's mother must have been medicated, because she hardly reacted at all.

I saw everyone from my class there. Mr. Conroy was there and so was Mrs. Evans. Amanda and Kelsey and Lexi and Emma were all there with their parents, but we didn't get a chance to talk, not that any of us could have anyhow. We were too busy crying. I think I used a whole box of tissues.

The flowers were unbelievable. When we left the graveyard it looked like a mountain of colored petals.

I feel so exhausted. So tired. I wish I could fall asleep and never wake up.

January 19

Dear Jo,

I told the therapist about the funeral, and she asked me what I thought of it. I said, "It was really sad, but it felt good to be with people who felt the same way I did."

"I think everyone feels awful about what happened to Leah. But it *has* touched you in a more personal way," she said.

"I bet whoever did this doesn't feel bad," I said.

"Maybe he does. Sometimes people have terrible sicknesses. Maybe part of him feels bad."

"I hope so. I hope he feels so bad he kills himself," I said.

"It's understandable that you feel this angry," she said.

"If it's so understandable, why do I have to come and talk to you all the time? I've been coming for months now and I don't feel any better at all. The only person who feels better is my mother, because she thinks I need you," I said.

She smiled and looked uneasy. Then she said, "You're here because you need to find a way to resolve your anger. That's the challenge."

"I'd be a lot less angry if I didn't have to waste my time talking to you," I said.

I thought she was going to tell me off after that, but she didn't. She just let me go early.

I wanted to tell her that catching Leah's killer would go a long way to helping me resolve my anger, but I was sure that would just land me with extra therapy time. She might think I have a revenge complex or something.

January 20

Dear Jo,

I went back to school today. Just before morning recess, Mr. Conroy read the best writing assignments out loud to the class. He read my poem last, after Gracie's short story about a dog who thought he was a budgie and Seth's fantasy story about a group of people who live on Pluto in rubber homes. At recess everyone was crying and said they really liked my poem. Lexi couldn't even talk she was so upset. I would have cried too, but I've been out of tears since the funeral. Apparently the school has brought in the grief counselors again, like they did when Leah first went missing.

I have a lot of work to catch up on, but Mom told

me not to worry about getting caught up right away, said Mr. Conroy would understand if I took a week or so to catch up. That made me want to laugh. I mean, I have about five months of work to catch up on, and I wouldn't be able to do it all, even if I wanted to.

January 21

Dear Jo,

Until today nobody knew I was doing this, but I've started crawling into bed with Molly again. I don't think Molly even knows I'm there because I crawl out again when the sun starts to come up. It feels better to have something warm and alive next to me while I think away the night. Anyhow, Mom found me in bed with Molly this morning. I actually fell asleep and didn't wake up until she came in. So now she won't let me watch the news anymore and doesn't want me reading about Leah's case in the papers. I know it's just because the details of what happened to her are going to start coming out and she doesn't want me to be even more upset. But I deserve to know the awful things that happened. I should have been watching out for Leah. I should have known something strange was going on.

I wonder if Mom's going to start giving me those little white sleeping pills again. I hope not, because they make me feel sick the whole next day. They make my skull feel about six inches thick. It's nice to be able to sleep, but I already feel weird enough without them. And I want to keep my mind as clear as possible. I want to be ready when that thought comes to me, that memory, that clue that is going to get the case moving.

January 22

Dear Jo,

Gus started saying "olly" for Molly and Molly thinks that's the best thing ever. She keeps going over and giving him big hugs and saying, "Say Molly, Gus. Say Molly." Then they end up on the floor wrestling and laughing. It's really cute to watch. She also tries to get him to say "Georgia," but he doesn't even try. And why should he? Georgia isn't even real.

I've been spending a lot of time with them lately, because I don't feel like going out and seeing my friends and because it makes Molly and Gus happy to have me around. Funny, but last year I hated having to be with them and had to be bribed to sit in the same room with them. Now I like them better than other people because they don't look at me funny or judge me. To them I'm just the same old moody Max.

January 23

Dear Jo,

I failed a math test and Mom is freaking out again. She's worried that my marks will slip back down, as if marks mean anything. It's funny how school grades are like a barometer for parents. If a kid gets an A, then everything is fine, even if that kid is messed up. Apparently, she was relieved I'd pulled my marks up to a D average on my last report card. Until this year, I'd never failed anything. In fact, my B- in French last year was my worst-ever mark. I would never have guessed I was capable of failing and not caring about failing. The only thing I worry about failing now is Leah again. I haven't had any more dreams about her, but I know there must be something in my head that can help Detective Lucas. I so badly want to *do* something now, to remember something. I know Detective Lucas can't call me every time he gets a lead or finds new evidence, but I wish I had *some* bit of news about what's going on.

Anyhow, Mom was so worried she went to meet with Mr. Conroy, and he said I'm very distracted in class. He says I'm not myself, as if he'd know. Mom agreed and said I haven't been myself for months. I know all this because Mom told me tonight when Dad was giving Molly and Gus a bath. She sat me down at the kitchen table for a "girl-to-girl" talk.

"I have to be honest, sweetheart. I'm afraid. I'm afraid you're going to go into another tailspin. I was so relieved to see you making progress. Christmas seemed to perk you up a bit. You were eating over the holidays and going out with us. But now you're so quiet again. I understand why, I do. I just don't want to let you slip too far away. I'm afraid I won't get you back this time."

I didn't answer. I just shrugged. What I really thought was that I hadn't ever really perked up at all. She was just too distracted to notice.

"You need to tell me how you're feeling. I need to know what's going on in that head of yours."

"What do you expect, Mom? It's like losing her all over again. Before I had some hope. But now there's nothing."

"I thought the funeral would bring some closure

for you."

"I don't want closure. I don't want to forget Leah. If I was dead, I wouldn't want people to forget me!"

"You don't have to forget her, honey. Nobody expects that. And please don't talk about being dead. It's like you're giving up altogether – on living, I mean. And I'm not going to let that happen. I know you're not going to want to hear this, but I made an appointment for us to see the therapist together tomorrow. Maybe she can suggest something, something to help us keep you ... keep you on track."

"I'm not a train, Mom! I'm a kid whose best friend is dead!"

Her voice caught in her throat, and she had to wait a minute to compose herself. I should have apologized for being so blunt, but I don't have any sorrys in me. Finally, she said, "I understand, but I also think there's more to it. Please just come with me tomorrow."

I rolled my eyes and left the room. It was my four gazillionth lecture from her.

Doesn't she understand? How can I care about anything, especially schoolwork, when my very best friend ever is dead because some creep she didn't even know, but who she trusted, killed her? How can I stop thinking about how it could have been me, or that if I'd been paying attention I could have stopped her from getting killed? How can I do schoolwork when Leah can't do anything anymore? At her funeral, the minister said she was a good student and a good athlete and had lots of friends, that she was loved by many. But what does it matter now that she's dead? What does it matter how fast she could run, or how many As she got, or how many people loved her? She can't go to sleepovers with us anymore or go horseback riding or tubing or eat way too much junk food and get a stomachache. She never gets to do anything again, so why should I? I won't be able to do anything or enjoy anything or think about anything until this guy is caught, and even then I might never be happy again.

January 24

Dear Jo,

I called Detective Lucas today. I had to find out if he had any leads, any clues, if there was anything they found at the crime scene that was going to help them catch Leah's killer. I had to hear hope in his voice, hear again that he wouldn't abandon the case. The good news is that he said there was some helpful forensic evidence on and around Leah's body, some identifying clues. The bad news is, he couldn't tell me what it is or anything about the case. I think he made me feel a little better. It helped just knowing somebody out there is still working on it.

January 26

Dear Jo,

Today Mom came with me to see the therapist. The therapist talked about me "touching base" with my parents once a day to discuss how I'm feeling. She also wants to see me more often so she can monitor me more closely. I swear, if there was a way, she'd monitor my dreams, my thoughts. Then she'd really have something to worry about. Talk about lack of privacy! If I don't seem to be coping, she said, she would recommend a more serious intervention, perhaps some medication. Just something to get me through this "rough period." Mom looked pleased that the therapist was taking it so seriously. I tried not to scream. The last thing I need is some drug clouding my brain. But with two against one, what choice did I have but to agree to talk to my parents every night before bed?

After Mom left, the therapist asked more questions about how I was feeling, and I told her I was bothered all over again by what happened to Leah. I know it's an obvious thing to say, but she expected me to say something and it took me five minutes to come up with it. I hate the sessions where we sit and listen to the clock ticking for an hour. I also hate the sessions where we discuss my attitude about living and dying. She said it was understandable that I was upset, but that I couldn't just give up living. So I said I understood what she was telling me, partly to make her feel better and partly just to get her to leave me alone. But between you and me (or, me and me), I don't really see why it matters if I live or not. I just haven't been able to put my head together enough to come up with a better plan than what I'm doing now.

The therapist really bugs me, and I don't think she has a clue. I wonder if she is so obvious with adults. Does she think I'm a stupid kid? Does she think I don't know exactly what she is going to say every minute? Does she think I can't tell myself all these same things? I could probably save Mom and Dad a heap of money by recording one session and playing it back to myself. She's the one making me crazy.

I wake up on therapy days with one more thing to dread, five more pounds on my shoulders. I think I've had a headache for seven months straight. And I don't know why I'm the only one who has to endure all this crap. Emma and Lexi and Amanda and Kelsey don't have to leave class to go and talk to some sniffly lady who probably hasn't even lost a pet before, not to mention a best friend. She tried to talk to me about the stages of grief one time, and I laughed out loud. I asked if there were badges. She didn't think it was funny at all. Leah would have thought it was funny though. Leah would have laughed herself silly over that one.

January 28

Dear Jo,

Molly has started to insist we call her Georgia and won't answer if we call her Molly. Somehow she has turned into her imaginary friend. So this morning I said to Mom, "She's the one who needs to see a shrink." Mom didn't get mad at me, but gave me that warning look and said, "Imaginary friends are very normal and you used to have one too."

"Really? What was her name?" I asked.

"Mark."

"I had an imaginary friend who was a boy?"

"Uh-huh."

"And you didn't worry about me?"

"Yes, I did. I took you to the doctor, and he sent me to a child development specialist, and she told me it was completely normal – that you'd grow out of it."

"And I did?"

"Yes, you did and so will Molly. So please just humor her for now."

I wonder if they say the same thing about me. *"Listen, Molly and Gus, Max is going through a rough patch right now, veering off the tracks. We all need to humor her for a while, agree with her, let her think we understand, pretend she isn't nuts."*

January 30

Dear Jo,

This morning, Mr. Conroy asked me to stay behind at recess again. Lexi gave me that "uh-oh" look as she left the class, and my head felt like it was about a million pounds on my neck. I was upset because I thought I'd failed another test and would have to miss recess to make it up, or that I was in for another teacher lecture, but he just wanted to tell me my poem got accepted into the tribute book for Leah. He said it's a really big accomplishment. He said lots of people would get to read my poem now and that her family would get to see how much I cared about Leah, how everyone cared about Leah, how she had become everyone's daughter, sister, niece, friend. I guess it's a nice thing if it will make her mother and father feel better, but I know that some poems and stories aren't going to make up for not having her alive anymore. Nothing can make up for that. About the only thing that can help a little will be to catch her killer. At least that's what I think.

February 4

Dear Jo,

The therapist is worried that I don't want to go out and do the things I used to. She means I should be spending time with my friends and going tobogganing and making plans with them for Valentine's Day. She said she was afraid I'd stopped caring about the things that are important to me.

I said, "I haven't stopped caring altogether, I'm just focusing on the things that really matter. Like, I care more about Gus and Molly now and less about schoolwork." I swear I could say any sort of garbage and she'd buy it.

"It's important to have your priorities straight. It shows a maturity that is rare in a twelve-year-old, but you still have to do the other things too, like schoolwork."

"But what does schoolwork matter if I'm going to get killed by some internet creep," I said. Sometimes it makes me feel better to play along.

"As long as you're careful, nothing is going to happen to you. You're smart and aware and safe. We've all learned a lot from what happened to Leah."

"But something else could happen. Someone could sneak into my room and steal me, or Molly, like they did to Elizabeth Smart or Cecilia Zhang."

"I know the media focuses on these cases and they are tragic, but the odds of something happening to you are very slim. Statistically speaking, Leah's case is extremely rare."

"I doubt statistics make Leah or her family feel

any better. They sure don't make me feel better. But thanks for trying," I said and walked out because the hour was up.

I know that was a rude thing to do, especially since she drives all the way to the school to see me each time, and I feel bad now. I know she is trying to help me and that everyone is worried about me, but I just can't help myself these days. My body seems to react before I can stop it. It's like a different person is inside me sometimes, doing and saying things that I later regret. I wish everyone would just leave me alone.

February 5

Dear Jo,

The best thing happened today and because it is so great and scary at the same time, I don't know how to feel. Detective Lucas came by our house again and this time, he had good news! After all this time, 2funE wrote back. They have no idea why 2funE chose to write now, and Detective Lucas warned me not to get too excited in case this isn't really Leah's killer. But they still want to pursue the lead. They think that he's been lying low all this time and is getting restless again. I'm so glad Detective

Lucas has been watching my Hotmail account all these months and that he never gave up hope. Here's what 2funE wrote:

> Hey Hottietoo. With Valentine's day approaching I couldn't help but write to you again. I miss you so much and I'm sorry for not writing all this time. My computer crashed and I got banned from the school computers for downloading MP3s. I know it's a totally lame excuse, but don't ever think you haven't been on my mind every day. I hope you haven't forgotten about me, or worse, found a new BF. SWAK 2funE

Detective Lucas was really happy that we were back in business. He took me over to the station so I could reply right away. This is what I wrote:

> Hey 2funE. I can't believe it's you! WOW! What a Valentine's surprise! I was so worried something bad happened to you. I mean, everything was so sweet

with us and then you just stopped
writing. I couldn't figure out if I said
something to make you mad or what. I've
been sad and lonely without you, but I
haven't found another BF. How could I?
I'm just happy to be back online with
you. I'm smiling ear to ear :{))))
What's been happening? How R U?
Hottietoo.

Part of me is afraid this is a false lead, that
someone is playing a sick joke, but who would know
my e-mail address? I only ever wrote to 2funE with it.
Detective Lucas said my online name was confidential information and that it was never on the news,
so right now I have to believe in this - it's all I have
to hold on to.

February 6

Dear Jo,

Today my parents surprised me. I told them I
thought I would sleep better and feel safer if we got a
dog. I guess after Elizabeth Smart was taken from her
home, her family bought two dogs. Apparently dogs

are the best security system you can get. At best I thought I would get a "maybe" answer to my suggestion, but they both looked really thoughtful and said it sounded like an excellent idea. Then Dad suggested we could go to the SPCA on the weekend and look for one. Mom didn't even object. She didn't say she expected me to be *responsible* for it or that she didn't need anything else to clean up after. She just nodded and agreed with Dad. I promised to walk it and feed it and take care of it. I've always wanted a dog.

Nothing back from 2funE yet.

February 7

Dear Jo,

As usual, the therapist wanted to keep talking about why I never go out anymore on the weekends and after school. She didn't say anything about me walking out on her last time, but she had my chair angled away from the door this time.

She said she'd been talking to Mom and that Mom said I wasn't going to the arena to free skate or to my friends' houses. That I hadn't been going to movies or the library. I wasn't even going uptown to buy junk food or new clothes. She told the therapist that my friends keep calling and inviting me out, but I never go anywhere except to school, and well, we all know that's not going so well either.

I said, "I have a responsibility to get Molly home after school, you know?"

"Yes, I'm aware you have a new routine and a way to earn some spending money on school nights. And your mother tells me you're doing a great job looking after Molly until she gets home from work. But I still think under normal circumstances, you'd be going out after dinner some nights, or out on the weekends with your friends, which you're not doing," she said.

She looked straight at me then, with her beady brown eyes that sometimes make her look like a mouse.

"I just feel better staying home. I feel safer and I can see that everyone I love is safe too. What's wrong with that?"

"Nothing," she said. "But from what I've heard about you, it's uncharacteristic. Your mom says you are normally very active and social and now you're not. She said you were on the volleyball team *and* the basketball team last year and that this year you didn't even try out. These sorts of changes in children's behavior, in anyone's behavior, signal that something deeper is happening and that makes your parents worry, makes me worry."

"It's no different than when I got grounded and hung around the house, only *then* nobody worried about me."

She didn't have an answer for me, I guess, because she said, "That's enough until our next session."

I shrugged and got up and left. But at least this time I didn't walk out on her. I meant to tell her about getting a dog, but I forgot.

Still nothing from 2funE. I have a bad feeling, like he senses something is up and will never write again. I'm afraid we lost our chance to catch him once and for all. I know I need to be optimistic and think positive thoughts, but it's hard when so much has gone wrong for so long.

February 9

Dear Jo,

Today Dad and I went to the SPCA to look for a dog. They had three dogs ready for adoption: a beagle named Trixie that was five years old, a puppy that was a husky-Lab cross and wasn't named, and a total mutt that was two years old and named Finn. I was relieved none of the dogs were named Max. Anyhow, it only took a second to choose and I picked Finn. He has longish hair and is black and tan in color. He isn't very big, only up to my knees, and he has the sweetest eyes ever. He's very gentle and kind to us because he came from a family with young kids. They really loved him, but moved to England and couldn't take him along because of the quarantine.

He's very polite and doesn't even snap at my hand when I feed him a treat like Amanda's dog does. Mom and Dad are letting him sleep in our bedroom and I already feel safer. I think he'll be a good watchdog too, because he'd only been home a few hours when the pizza delivery guy rang the bell and he barked like crazy. Right now he's lying beside my bed with his legs in the air, barking like he's having a dream. Everyone likes him, but I think he likes me best, and not just because I feed and walk him and don't climb all over him like Gus does. Goodnight, Finn.

February 10

Dear Jo,

Guess what? Detective Lucas stopped by after school to say 2funE wrote back at last! He printed off the reply and brought it to me:

> Hey Hottietoo. I'm so relieved you understand. U R the best GF a guy could ever hope for. You don't have to worry about me leaving you ever again because I got a new computer – a laptop – that I bought myself. It's totally wicked. I love it and I can download as many MP3s as I want to now. Guess what else? I got a job! It's just at a gas bar pumping gas, but it means I have some money to spend and I want to spend it on you. Maybe I could send you something special for Valentines? Besides my love, I mean. I am such a happy guy right now. I was worried you would have forgotten about me and the thought of that made me feel sick. AML 2funE

I don't know whether to be relieved or disgusted. Of course, I'm relieved he wrote back and I hope it's the right guy so we can nail him. But he totally disgusts me. Whenever I picture his face and read his words, think about him being with Leah, I feel like puking. Luckily I have time to compose something before I have to send my reply. Detective Lucas is going to pick me up after dinner and take me to the police station so we can write back.

Later

Tonight on the way over to the police station, the Goo Goo Dolls were playing *Give a Little Bit* on the radio. I love that song and said so. Detective Lucas smiled and said something about it being a classic from when he was a kid. I didn't know what he meant, and I didn't want to ask and look stupid in front of him, so I just agreed. We talked for a while about music, and he asked me what my favorite band was. I said Avril Lavigne.

"She's got a good voice."

"Yeah. She was Leah's favorite too. Who do you like?"

"A bit of everything. I like the Goo Goo Dolls, Matchbox 20, Jack Johnson, and a bunch of the old stuff your Dad probably listens to."

"The Eagles?"

"Oh yeah."

"The Rolling Stones?"

"Uh huh."

"*Pink Floyd*?"

"Absolutely."

"Well, at least you listen to some good stuff too."

He laughed, just a little. "So, do you have any ideas about what you want to write to 2funE?"

"I used to complain to him about my parents and Molly and Gus a lot, so I guess I should keep doing that. I also used to tell him about what I did with my friends. He was really interested in my friends. I didn't use their real names though. I had code names for all of them. So I should make up something I've done with them lately. It's weird to think some grown-up cares what I did on the weekend with my friends. I mean, when I thought I was writing to another kid, it seemed so normal. But now, well, it just feels creepy."

"We'll get this guy, and you won't ever have to

write him again. I promise."

After he said that, I just knew Detective Lucas thought 2funE was Leah's killer. He warned me before not to get my hopes too high, but I think that's just because he doesn't want me to be disappointed if he's wrong. People don't think I can handle another big disappointment, and to tell you the truth, I'm not sure I can either. But his confidence is giving me some hope again, and it feels good to have that feeling for a change.

February 11

Dear Jo,

Today on the way to the police station, Detective Lucas and I talked about getting me hooked up to the internet at home. It was my idea, and I was afraid he'd react like Mom and Dad, but he didn't.

"Once we really got going, I used to write 2funE more than once a day," I said and then felt embarrassed.

"Oh yeah? How often?" Detective Lucas asked.

"Usually I'd write before school, then at lunch, and then after school too. And at bedtime, through Leah of course."

"That's a lot. Did he answer every time?"

"Yeah. There was always something waiting. That's why I kept writing. It was addictive."

"I guess he must be on the computer a lot."

"I guess. But the thing is, once we get back into a routine, I know he'll start expecting the same."

"You're thinking like a detective already." He smiled over at me then, and it felt really good to be treated like a grown-up for once.

"So anyway, I was thinking that it's going to start getting busy for you, driving me back and forth so much."

"I wouldn't mind, but I'm not sure your mother would like it. I had to work hard to convince her she didn't need to come with us once a day."

"She worries a lot."

"It's her job."

"I guess," I said.

"It might make the neighbors suspicious if they see you leaving with me three or four times a day," he said.

"I have an idea, but I bet you won't like it. And I know Mom definitely won't like it."

"What's that?"

"Get me the internet at home. We could move Dad's computer out to the living room or something, just so Mom could keep a close eye on me. I swear I wouldn't do anything but write e-mails to 2funE like I'm supposed to."

"You wouldn't feel uncomfortable with your parents there? I'm sure they'll be more interested in what you're writing if you're sitting right in front of them."

"I already thought of that. No. I think I can handle it. I'll just think of it as creative writing. Besides, I might feel more natural being at home."

"Okay. If that's what you want. I'll talk to your parents when we get you home. I bet we can get them to see things our way."

I loved the way he said that, *our* way. As if we were a team.

When we got home, Detective Lucas had a word with Mom and Dad, and within five minutes they agreed to get a broadband cable connection. I should have it in a couple of days. Of course, Mom didn't look very pleased at first, but Detective Lucas promised he'd be monitoring my account from the police station and would see everything going out and coming back. He promised to give them regular updates.

February 15

Dear Jo,

We have the computer in the living room, and Mom has insisted on reading all of my e-mails before I send them, just to be safe. You should have seen her face when she read this:

> Hey 2funE. How's my BF? I'm sorry if you were sad thinking I might have forgotten you. How could I ever forget about you? I never gave up hope. I knew you'd write me back eventually. As Pumba says, it's time to put our behinds in the past. Not too much has happened here. My parents are still the world's biggest drag ;-) Also I'm doing well at school. Did you have a good Valentine's Day? I did because I've heard from you. BTW, I hope you aren't going to hate me but I got braces. They don't look so bad and the orthodontist says I won't have to wear them for too long. TOY. LYWAMH.

She said, "What does all that punctuation at the end of that sentence mean?"

"It's a wink and a smile."

"What's BF?"

"Boyfriend."

"And BTW?"

"By the way."

"And TOY?"

"Thinking of you."

"LYWAMH?"

"Love you with all my heart."

"Why don't you just use real words?"

"This is just the way it's done. It's more fun."

"If you put this much effort into your school-work, you'd be a straight A student again."

"Whatever," I said.

When Detective Lucas came by earlier to help set up the computer, I found out that he isn't even from Port Hope. He's been staying up here to work on this case because he's part of a special unit that investigates crimes involving children. His specialty is internet crimes. I'm sort of going to miss seeing him every day, now that I can write from home. I don't know why, but I feel like I connect with him, like he understands me. Plus he's really easy to be with. He never disapproves of anything or is shocked by anything I say. And he never tries to correct me or lecture me.

P.S. Finn definitely likes me best. He always sleeps by my bed and waits by the door for me to get home from school. Then he jumps all over me and whines until I get down on the floor to say "Hi" to him. Tonight Molly was sad because he doesn't like her best, but I said he liked her second best, then got him to lick her face goodnight and told her it was a dog kiss. So she went to bed happy.

February 16

Dear Jo,

Tonight I was composing an e-mail when Dad came home. He asked how it was going and came to read over my shoulder. I know they are trying to give me the space I need to write, yet keep a close eye on me too. This is what I was responding to:

> Hey Hottietoo GF. I can't beleive you remembered that I love The Lion King.

It's a classic. Hakuna Matata, you know? Let's not worry about anything now that we have each other again. I can't beleive I was ever worried that you'd forget about me. You make me feel so specail. I'm sure your braces look good on you. How could they not? I bet you are gorgeous from head to toe and every-thing in between :) Every night I imagine what you look like and what it would be like to be with you. Tell me again what you look like, just so I can fall asleep with a picture of you in my head. LYWAMH.

After I sent my reply, Detective Lucas called to tell me I'm doing a great job writing my e-mails.

"I can't thank you enough for helping us, Max. We couldn't do it without you. We needed someone who already knew this guy. He would have smelled an imposter in a second."

"I'm doing it for Leah. I want this guy caught and put in jail. I wish he was already in jail. When do you think I should try to set up a meeting?"

"Don't rush it or he'll get suspicious. As long as

we have him online we're in good shape. And we're collecting more and more information all the time. I think the best thing to do is wait for *him* to suggest a meeting again. We'll just play it by ear. He's bound to do it soon. He'll be getting restless."

"Are you sure he won't lure someone else before we get to him or just grab some poor girl off the street?"

"We're doing all we can to be sure that doesn't happen. We're monitoring all his known e-mail accounts and watching the chat rooms he likes, but we can never be sure. As for grabbing someone, I don't think it's his style. It could backfire on him, and he seems to need to have complete control. But that's for me to worry about. You just need to worry about yourself and keep writing those e-mails."

To tell the truth I get really nervous writing to 2funE. I'm afraid I'm going to give something away. I want to tell him how much I hate him and what a creep he is and I have to work really hard to be calm and sound natural. It takes me three or four drafts before I'm happy with what I've got. I could never do this in person or on the phone. I'm not a very good actor. But I think I'm a pretty good writer. Whenever I get scared that he's going to catch on I have to remind myself he doesn't know me, he doesn't know I knew Leah, he doesn't even know I'm from Port Hope. When he brings it up, I'll have to agree to meet him in the city. If I mention Port Hope, he might get suspicious.

February 18

Dear Jo,

It didn't take long for 2funE to get to the point, only thirteen days to be exact, if you can believe it. He must be getting restless, just like Detective Lucas predicted. Today he suggested we should meet, that we've waited so long – almost a year – to finally see each other. He said he's lost so much sleep thinking about me that he's going to be a wreck if it doesn't happen soon. I bet he has no idea what it's really like to be a wreck and not be able to sleep. I so want to get this guy. I told Detective Lucas I was ready to nail him. This is what I wrote tonight:

> Hey 2funE BF. I think it would be great to meet. FINALLY. Can you believe we've known each other so long? You're right. We've waited long enough. I feel I know you better than I know myself and

I can't wait to see you in person, to look in your eyes and hold your hand. I could meet you at the Milltown Mall. It's not too far for me to go after school or on a weekend. I'm so excited. I can feel my heart pounding. When can we meet? TOY. IWLYF.

PS Don't worry, I promise I will never forget about you.

Here's what I really want to say:

> You scumbag. I can't wait until your are behind bars for the rest of your life and then I hope you never have a chance to walk down the street again. You don't ever deserve to feel the sun on your face or the grass under your toes. You took something so special from me. You probably don't even have any idea what you crushed. You probably didn't even take the time to get to know Leah before you killed her. I will never be able to understand what you have done, because you are sick in the head.

But I will never forget Leah and when this is all over, I'm never going to think about you again. That's a promise.

February 23

Dear Jo,

I don't think 2funE has any idea what is going on. I think I've totally sucked him in. That's the irony of it all. We've suckered each other. Only I know what's going on this time, and he doesn't.

> Oh Hottietoo GF, you are making me the happiest guy in school. My freinds keep asking why I have a stupid grin on my face :)))))))))) but I can't help it. I looked back to see when we first met and it was the end of March. I would like to wait for our one-year aniversary, but that is toooooo long. I just can't wait a day longer than necesary. Can you meet next Saturday at the food court, by the potted trees? I have hockey practice in the morning but I could be there by one. I'll be wearing

my blue school jacket. Go Griffins! What will you be wearing? And you can call me Brad when you see me, that's my real name. SWAK. LYF. PS Do you have a cell phone number so I can call if we don't find each other?

Brad is the same name muscleboy gave to Leah when they agreed to meet, so I'm feeling even more sure that this is the right guy. I mean, what are the chances that two different internet predators would use the same fake name?

February 24

Dear Jo,

Detective Lucas came over to our house tonight so we could plan our next steps. He told me that since 2funE told me his name, I should tell him mine too, or I should tell him a fake one, to keep him hooked. I thought pretty hard before I decided to go with Judee.

"Why Judee?" he asked.

"Because I'm betraying him."

Then we sat down together while I composed this e-mail:

> My sweetest Brad. I love that name, it sounds so strong. I can't believe this is going to happen at last. I have been waiting so long to meet you in person. I'm all set for Saturday and I don't even have to make up a lie about where I'm going because my parents are taking my little brother and sister to see Blue's Clues (there's a live tour, if you can believe it) and will be out all afternoon. I'll be wearing a red sweater and a red-and-white striped scarf. When you see the sweater, you'll know why I wore it just for you ,-). I won't be able to sleep at all Friday night. I'm already nervous, in an excited kind of way. Maybe we can catch a movie in the afternoon. BTW, my name is Judee. Don't ask, it's just more proof that my parents are super weird. LYWAMH. PS Please don't make me wait too long! I'll definitely be there waiting and you'll know me when you see me. I know it's outrageous, but I don't have a cell phone. Like I've said a million times, my parents are from the dark ages.

Even I could see the brilliance in my response. Maybe I *should* be a writer when I grow up! Either that or a professional liar. I can come up with lies when I have to, without even pausing. Or maybe I could be a detective and catch the liars. I think I might have a knack for this. When he read it over, Detective Lucas told me I was brilliant. He said having my parents out for the afternoon was a stroke of genius, said it would lull 2funE into a false sense of security, put him off guard, make him a little careless, hopefully, because he will think there won't be anyone at home waiting for me, that nobody will notice that I'm missing until almost dinnertime.

"And what made you suggest a movie?" he asked.

"He suggested it before. Besides, we hadn't made any plans yet and it seemed fake. I mean, who'd go to meet someone for the first time without making plans about how to spend the afternoon?"

"Good thinking," he said.

"Thanks. So now what?" I asked.

"Now comes the tricky part. We need to talk to your parents."

"About what?"

"About how I envision this whole sting happening," he said.

I didn't ask for details, but when I hit send, I felt a chill run up the back of my neck. Detective Lucas went and asked Mom and Dad if he could talk to them in the living room – said he had something serious to discuss with all of us together. They had already put Gus and Molly to bed, so they came in and sat on the couch beside me. We looked up at him with expectant faces. He took a deep breath, let the room go silent and explained how he wants me to help catch 2funE in person, to be part of the actual police sting. He told us how the sting would involve me going to the mall where 2funE and I planned to meet and waiting for 2funE to approach. Once 2funE calls me by the name Judee and starts talking about Brad, the police will know he's the right guy and will pounce on him. They're confident he will find an excuse to get me out to his car, but they won't let things go that far.

I couldn't believe what I was hearing, but I didn't dare say "No." I mean, I guess I sort of knew Detective Lucas wanted me to help with this step, but he's never spelled it out before. I never thought about having to actually face 2FunE in person. I tried not to let my fear get in the way. I knew I'd have time to worry about it later and that I just had to agree in order to keep the momentum going, to get him behind bars once and for all.

I was pretty sure Mom was going to freak. But she didn't. She totally surprised me. She spoke quietly and rationally. I could hardly believe she was my mother.

"I have to admit that I feel manipulated. When this all started, I thought we were only agreeing to letting Max write a few e-mails. Now you want us to let her come face-to-face with a criminal, a *murderer*. I can't change where we are in the process or how we got here, but I have to tell you, I didn't think it would come to this," she said.

"I'm sorry you feel this way. I didn't plan it. And I don't want you to think I was trying to trick you. But this is how things have worked out, where our investigation has brought us, and we don't want to miss this opportunity," Detective Lucas said.

"I appreciate the importance of this step, this sting, as you call it. I do. And I loved Leah almost as much as I do my own kids, so I do want to see this guy put away where he can't hurt any more children. But how can you guarantee that Maxine won't get hurt in all of this?" she asked.

"We'll have her wired and monitored and surrounded by undercover police. She'll never be more than a short distance away from me, and we plan to have your husband nearby too, for extra support. I would never put Max in danger," Detective Lucas said.

"And why Maxine? Why can't you use an undercover cop to pose as this Judee character?"

"We've only got one shot at this. This guy is a pro. It's taken us nine months to get this close to him, and we have no solid leads on who he is, I mean who he *really* is. If we put in a fake, he's going to spot it a mile away. I'm sure he's going to be watching for something suspicious. I can't bear to see him get away. We need him to approach Max and blow his cover. We need to hear him use the names so we have proof it's not a misunderstanding. But we won't let Max get too close, she won't be in any danger of being abducted or hurt."

"I just don't know," Mom said, shaking her head. She looked at Dad and asked, "What do you think?"

He took her hand and held it for a moment before he spoke.

"I think it's the scariest thing we can ever imagine letting one of our children do. But I know if I was Leah's Dad, I'd need us to say 'Yes.'"

"Mom, please? Please let me do this for Leah, for *me*," I said finally, in a quiet voice.

She didn't say "Yes," and she didn't say "No," but she nodded and started to cry. Then she left the room.

I'm supposed to be sleeping, but of course it's really hard to stop my mind from racing with so many thoughts. I've even tried the deep breathing techniques I learned from the therapist last fall, but nothing is helping. Not even writing is making me the least bit sleepy. How can I possibly stop thinking about how we're going to get this guy, about how I'm going to come face-to-face with Leah's killer?

February 25

Dear Jo,

Detective Lucas went to the city today to start working out the logistics and to get his team together for Saturday. On his way out of town, he dropped by to talk to me. He said there are a lot of details to work out and many things to put in place.

"Are you going to have enough time?" I asked.

"Don't worry about that. I've got it covered. I've been trained to pull off these sorts of operations in very little time. Guess what we're calling it?"

"You don't really name these things."

"Sure we do."

"They only do that in movies and on TV."

"I'm telling the truth. We always name our operations. It helps keep everyone focused and makes everything more confidential. So take a guess."

"I dunno. Operation Leah?"

He shook his head.

"Operation Internet Predator?"

He shook his head.

"Operation 2funE?

He shook his head.

"I give up, just tell me."

"We've called it Operation Max."

"Really?"

"Scout's honor."

"Shouldn't it be Operation Leah?"

"No. This is about the person who is going to catch her killer, and that's you."

"What should I do in the meantime?"

"The same as you have been doing. Just write and talk about how great it will be to meet on Saturday. I'll be in touch by phone and I'll be monitoring the Hotmail account. You have my cell number if you need it. And don't be afraid to use it. I'm available twenty-four hours a day. So call me, especially if you start to get nervous, even if you just want to talk."

"Okay."

"Promise?"

"Promise."

"I don't want you to worry about anything. We need you in good shape for Saturday. You're the lead actor, the MVP, if you know what I mean."

"Yeah, I know what you mean, but still, we can't forget this is about Leah too."

"Don't worry. We haven't forgotten Leah. But she's lucky she has a friend who cares so much, who's willing to get involved. You deserve a little recognition."

I couldn't speak right then because my throat tightened and my eyes filled up with tears. I think Detective Lucas noticed because he didn't wait for me to reply. He kept on talking.

"I'll be back up Friday to go over every detail with you and your parents. You'll have lots of opportunities to ask questions and memorize your part. Then you'll need to get to bed early and get a good sleep. I'll drive you and your parents down to the city Saturday morning."

"Okay."

"You're gonna do great. I can't think of anyone else who could pull this off," he said. I could tell he was happy.

It's hard to describe how I'm feeling now. I'm nervous, of course. But I'm relieved too, relieved to be finally doing something, to be so close to catching Leah's killer. I'm scared and sad and anxious. But the good news is I am feeling *something* again. I didn't realize until just now, but I've been numb the last few weeks, and it feels good to have emotions pumping through me again.

February 26

Dear Jo,

Only three more sleeps until the most dangerous day of my life. I can't believe that a year ago I was taking a babysitting course and arguing with Mom about when I deserved to be paid for watching Molly and Gus and when I should do it for free. So much has changed in a year, I hardly know who I am anymore. Leah wouldn't even recognize me.

I'm having a hard time concentrating at school, but not just because of the regular stuff. I can't stop thinking about Saturday and what it will be like to be wired up and have all those people counting on me. I keep wondering how creepy 2funE will be and how hard it will be not to run away from him. I bet he's really gross and smelly. What if he tries to touch me? I mean, I know they won't let him hurt me, but I don't want him to get too close or I might puke and blow my cover. I just have to keep remembering why I'm doing this. I have to keep remembering it's for Leah. I can't let her down, not this time. This is my chance to help put this guy away.

February 27

Dear Jo,

Lexi called tonight and asked if I wanted to go to the movies on Saturday. She said the new Pixar movie is opening, and she got tickets online. Lexi knows I love Pixar movies so I'm sure that's why she got the tickets. They're all trying their best to include me and get me out of the house. Good thing

I've been such a hermit lately or she might have been suspicious when I said, "No thanks."

I haven't been able to tell anyone about Operation Max, not even Molly. I've had to go to school and see the therapist and try to act normal. I've been doing so much acting lately that it's hard to remember what "normal" is - it's hard to remember who I am. Mostly I just keep quiet because then I can't say anything I'm not supposed to.

Mom just tucked Molly into bed so I put my headphones on and am under my covers again. Right now I'm listening to Pink, *Stupid Girls*, and thinking about Leah. She would have loved this song. She hated girls who pretended to be stupid, just to be popular. I wonder if Leah is watching all of this. I wonder if she is looking down and cheering for me? I like to think she is. I like to think she sees how much I'm doing to get this guy so she knows how much I miss her. I like to think she'll give me the courage I need. I have to think that or I'll chicken out.

February 28

Dear Jo,

Tonight Detective Lucas spent two hours

coaching me on how to stand casually, but not too casually, because he says 2funE will watch me for a while before he approaches me, just to be sure I'm not there to bait him. He says I need to look as if I'm waiting for someone, but that I can't look too nervous. I should have taken drama last year as an elective. He's been really encouraging. He also showed me a floor plan of the mall and where all the other police officers will be positioned. He showed me where he would be in the CD store and where Dad would be in the food court. He also showed me a video of the mall and pictures too, so I would feel familiar with it, just in case 2funE does something we aren't expecting and I have to improvise.

Once 2funE approaches me, I have to talk to him long enough for him to explain why he's not a sixteen-year-old boy and why I need to leave the mall with him. Then I have to make like I am going to leave with him and go to his car. As we are about to exit the mall, the police are going to pounce on him, and Dad's going to grab me and get me someplace safe.

I can't believe I'm going to do this. They're going to dress me up to look older because 2funE thinks I'm almost fifteen, not almost thirteen. I have to wear a bra and pad it out and everything. It's going to be so embarrassing. Luckily, my sweater is stretchy enough to get over all the equipment and my fake chest. It's also a good thing they have a female detective who works with disguises to help me.

I know I am as prepared as I can be, but still I can barely sleep – I keep thinking of everything that can go wrong.

march 1

Dear Jo,

You have no idea how nervous I am. We are on the highway, just approaching the city. I can see the high-rises in the distance and there are twelve lanes of traffic whipping past us. We're going to drop Mom at Aunt Laurie's and we're going to call her as soon as everything is over. I feel a little bad that she can't be there, but I know she'd make me more nervous, and that wouldn't be good. Detective Lucas said we've only got one chance. He's been at the mall, setting up cameras and getting his people ready. They're already in place, right this very minute, just in case 2funE is stalking the place early.

Nobody in Port Hope knows what's going on. Not even Mrs. Barnes from next door who is watching Molly and Gus. She thinks I'm going to see a special orthodontist about getting a retainer so that I can get my braces off. That was my own invention too, because Mrs. Barnes is always asking me about my braces and how they feel and when they're coming off.

I'm eating gummy worms (even though the dentist told me not to) to calm my stomach. I know it sounds weird, but I couldn't face eating breakfast, and Mom said I had to have something in my stomach. So I asked for gummy worms and presto! I got them. It feels good to have something sweet to eat. Leah loved gummy worms as much as I do. We had a contest once to see who could put the most in their mouth. It was just the two of us, and we were in her bedroom trying not to laugh too loud and wake up her parents because it was after midnight. Of course she won, but she suffered for it the next day because she had the runs. Who knew you could get the runs from eating too many gummy worms?

We just dropped off Mom and she was trying her best not to cry. She asked one last time why they couldn't use someone else, someone older. Detective Lucas was very patient. He explained that I'm the one with all the information in my head. He said if 2funE wants to sit down and have a conversation, just to be cautious, I'd be the only one who could respond appropriately. Then he told her for the gazillionth time that I'd be safe and well-protected and not to worry. Then Aunt Laurie took her away so she wouldn't upset me.

It's very still in the car now. Dad isn't saying much and neither am I. I think we're both as scared as Mom, but too chicken to admit it. Detective Lucas just put Avril Lavigne on and that is already making me feel better. I *am* feeling like an MVP, and to tell you the truth, it feels kind of nice. Dad has started cracking his knuckles. Mom hates when he does that.

Detective Lucas said we'd be at the police station in a few minutes. That's where I'm going to get in disguise. Then we're going to drive over to the mall together in a surveillance van. I think my heart is going to pound right through my rib cage. I wish it was already over.

I am *so* scared. I peed before I left the house, but I have to pee again. This is worse than waiting at the start of a race. I'm not sure I can do this. But I have to. I've got to try those deep breathing exercises. I just wish my hands weren't so sweaty. What if 2funE wants to hold hands and notices how nervous I am?

What if my face starts going red when he talks to me? What if my voice freezes? He might take one look at me and bolt, and then they'd miss him. Oh God. I've got to get a grip. Breathe, Max, breathe.

Oh crap. We're pulling into the parking lot at the police station. I've got to go now. Wish me luck. This is for you, Leah.

Later

I still feel sick whenever I think about what happened today. I'm not even sure I can write about it. But I'll try while it's still fresh in my memory.

It took about an hour to get me all rigged with wires and surveillance equipment, and then for the makeup lady to do my hair and makeup. When I was finished Dad looked sad and said, "It's a good thing we left your mother with Aunt Laurie or she'd be dragging you home. You look so ... so ... so grown up." Then he tried to hug me, but the detective told him not to crush the wires.

When I looked in the mirror I couldn't believe it was me either. It felt like I was dressed up for Halloween or something. In a way it was better to look so different because then I didn't feel like Maxine Marie Lemay. I felt like Avril Lavigne or Lindsay Lohan or Pink or someone much much older. I guess I felt like Judee.

I drove with Detective Lucas and Dad to the basement of the mall, and that's where we had to split up. I almost cried. I was really shaky and nervous. But I put it all out of my mind and tried to get into character. Detective Lucas and Dad went to take their places by the food court. Before he left, Detective Lucas promised there would be police officers all around me, even if I didn't recognize them.

The female detective who wired me, escorted me to a back entrance, let me walk out by the washrooms, and told me exactly where to go. But I totally knew where I was and where I was going because of all the prep work we had done. I walked alone through the mall the way I was supposed to, even stopped and looked at some bracelets in a jewelry store the way we planned. I could see the clerk was really the undercover cop I had met earlier, and that made me feel safer. Then I made my way to the food court and hung out by the potted trees, trying to look at least fifteen. I waited and glanced around casually for a few minutes, then started checking my watch just often enough to look expectant, but not too often in case I looked suspicious.

I tried not to be obvious, but I could see Dad a few tables away pretending to eat tacos and read the paper, and I could see Detective Lucas dressed in street clothes and looking at CDs near the entrance of the music store, exactly where he said he would be. Whenever a teenage boy went by, I pretended to be ready to meet Brad, but really, I was scanning the faces of the men and wondering which of them was the murderer, which one was 2funE.

I'd been standing there waiting for about ten minutes when an old man came up to me. He was old enough to be my dad's Dad. He had grey hair and the wrinkliest skin I've ever seen. I couldn't believe he could be the person who killed Leah. He didn't look strong enough to kill a fly. Still, I stayed in my role as Judee when he spoke.

"Excuse me, dear. Do you know where the bookstore is? I've been around the whole mall four times and I still can't find it."

My stomach flopped because I had no idea where the bookstore was. It wasn't something we'd reviewed. I felt like I was about to fail the biggest test of my life. I swallowed hard and opened my mouth, and suddenly this brilliant lie flew out.

"To tell you the truth, I don't buy a lot of books. But you could check on the map over there," I said and pointed to a display by the glass doors.

"Of course, that's what I'll do. Thank you muchly."

He tottered off, and I waited in horror, wondering if that had been it, if it was over, if I'd blown it, if 2funE had figured out our scam. But I caught Detective Lucas's eyes through the window of the music store and he signaled that everything was okay, that I should stay calm and keep waiting.

As it was, I didn't notice him approach, he was just suddenly at my side. My heart pounded so hard when I heard his voice, I was sure he'd be able to hear the thumping. But maybe he just thought I was excited about meeting him. He didn't look at all like the police drawing. He'd grown a goatee and was wearing a New York Yankees ball cap backward. He wasn't even creepy – he was kind of cute for an older guy. I wouldn't have been afraid of him at all if I didn't know what he was capable of. He was dressed in blue jeans and a leather jacket, and he was clean-cut. He even smelled good, and I could tell he had shaved that day.

He didn't hesitate once I noticed him. He said, "Judee?"

I tried to look surprised that he knew my name.

"Yeah, that's me."

"Are you waiting to meet Brad?"

"Yeah, he's my friend."

"Brad's my son. My oldest son. He couldn't make it. He had an accident at hockey practice this morning. And he was really upset about missing you. He said he didn't want you to think he'd stood you up."

"Is he okay?"

"He's just at the doctor's getting some stitches. Nothing too serious. He said he has his cell phone on if you want to call him."

Detective Lucas and I had gone over some different scenarios that 2funE might use to lure me outside, but we hadn't come up with this one. Still, I knew it didn't matter what the excuse was – the thing was he'd want me to leave with him. So I tried my best to keep calm and play along.

"I don't have a cell phone," I said, knowing I'd already told "Brad" that in an e-mail.

"You can use mine," he said and then patted his jacket pocket. "Shoot. I left it in the car. I'm always doing that. Come on and I'll let you use it. I've got his number programmed in. I can't even remember what it is any more." Then he smiled, and I thought about how he would have smiled the same way at Leah. I wondered what excuse he gave her. He was so friendly and easy-going, so straightforward and non-threatening, I'm not surprised Leah fell for his act.

"Well if you don't mind, that would be great," I said and followed at his side. We walked together toward the glass doors, and he didn't seem nervous at all. He smiled down at me in a fatherly way and didn't force the conversation. I could barely make my legs move, and I tried to keep in my role – tried not to think about what he did to Leah and that he was the last one to see her alive. I knew he was falling right into our trap, and my hands got really sweaty. But I concentrated on breathing and walking. When we were almost at the outside doors, it was my turn to lie.

"Wait, I left my purse on that bench back there."

We turned together to look, and there it was, a red purse bought that morning and stuffed with tissues, like a prop in a play.

"It will only take me a second. I'll be right back."

I knew I had him in exactly the right place, so I looked up and smiled shyly. Then I ran back for the purse. By the time I turned around to look, he was face down on the floor with ten policemen pointing guns at him and another two on top of him. He was yelling and screaming and demanding to know what was going on. His face was red and the veins in his neck were popping out like he was choking. His arms were twisted back like they were broken and every time he struggled, a police officer pushed a knee between his shoulder blades until he yelped.

He kept saying, "You've got the wrong guy, I know that girl. She's my son's friend. I haven't done anything wrong. Let me go. Let me *go*."

He even yelled out to me. "Judee! Judee! Tell them they've made a mistake. Brad said to tell you he loves you."

That's when I felt weak and my legs buckled, but Dad was there with his arms around me, and he and another police officer helped me away as fast as they could. I wanted to look back, just so he could see me, but I couldn't. They had me around the corner and outside before I had a chance. By then, a crowd had started to gather, and the undercover officers were telling people to stay back.

The fresh air felt good, and I gulped it back like water. My eyes were flowing with tears and I was trembling. I leaned against the wall and slid to the ground. Then I felt the gummy worms coming back up my throat. Dad patted my back while I threw up all over the pavement, and the police officer handed me some tissues and a bottle of water. I tried to drink away the bad taste, but even the water came right back up so that my mouth tasted sour again. I tried to breathe, but I couldn't. I just I heaved and heaved. I didn't think my stomach would ever be empty.

Finally I was able to walk, and we made our way to the van. Dad didn't let go of me, even for one second, and he put his sweatshirt over my shoulders to help me get warm. It was such a relief to sit down inside the van, so I asked if it was okay if I lay down. The police gave me a coat as a blanket and Dad sat so I could use his lap as a pillow.

"Are you okay?" Detective Lucas asked as soon as he climbed in the van.

I couldn't speak right then, so I just nodded.

"Are you sure?" He kneeled beside me.

"Yeah. I'm just, like, really tired. You know?"

He took my hand and squeezed it, then said,

"Max, I'm very proud of you. You were great. You were so brave. You should be proud of yourself ."

"Where is he?" I asked.

"On the way to the police station. He's hand-cuffed and is with two very strong police officers. They're going to hold him until I get you back home."

My eyes were filling up with tears again, and even I couldn't figure out why. They came unexpect-edly and in a flood, and there was nothing I could do to stop them.

"Are you sure you're going to be okay?" he asked in a super soft voice.

"I dunno. I'm glad it's over and we got the guy, but Leah's still dead."

Nobody said anything for a few minutes, and I concentrated on breathing. I closed my eyes and saw Leah in my mind. It was one of my favorite memories of her – the time she sneaked into my bedroom so she could be the first person to say Happy Birthday to me. It was the year I turned ten. She'd trudged all the way over in the snow before school. And she had a present for me. Her eyes were sparkling and she was so excited she made me open it before I even sat up. It was a small silver statue of a fairy sitting on a mushroom. There was a key hidden in the fairy's wings that opened a secret compartment. The key was silver too, with three red stones embedded in it. Inside was a letter she'd written about what a special friend I was, and how I always made her smile. She'd covered the letter with happy-face stickers. She made me promise not to tell the others so that they wouldn't get jealous. I never did. I still have the fairy on the shelf in my room. I still have the letter too. And I've been wearing the key on a chain around my neck since the day she went missing.

Detective Lucas cleared his throat, and I opened my eyes.

"How are you feeling?" he asked

"As good as can be expected. I think I'll miss seeing you though. You've been around a lot lately."

"Don't worry about that. You'll still see me."

"Will you come back up to Port Hope?"

"Absolutely."

"Promise?"

"Scout's honor."

"Were you ever really a Boy Scout?"

"No," he said, and we both smiled a little.

When I was feeling better, we called Mom. I told her I was okay. A police officer went to get her so that we could all meet at the station to debrief. When she saw me she flew across the room and hugged me so hard I thought I'd snap in two. It was easy to tell I'd been crying because my mascara was smudged, and after she looked at my face she threw a dirty look at Dad and then at Detective Lucas. But I could tell she was more relieved than angry, and once we were finished debriefing, it didn't take long before she was just plain proud of me.

We're not allowed to talk about this to anyone until after 2funE has been put in jail for good, because Detective Lucas says they still have to investigate more and go to trial and all of that. But my part is done and I'm glad. Now I'm back home with Finn, who is sitting at my feet right this very moment. I'm still feeling like an MVP because Dad and Mom keep asking if there is anything I need or anything they can get me. I haven't even bothered to ask again for my own room or contact lenses *or* to keep the internet.

I hate to brag, but I *am* proud of myself. I know what I did today was probably the hardest thing I'll ever do, and I did it perfectly. I didn't let anyone down. I didn't let Detective Lucas or myself or Leah down. I hope her parents find out what I did. I want them to know how much I miss her, but what can I say that would mean anything to them? I mean, they lost their only kid. But maybe if they find out what I had to do to catch Leah's killer, they'll understand how much I wanted to help. Even if I couldn't bring her back, I did something worthwhile.

March 5

Dear Jo,

Today Mr. Conroy gave me *Leah's Book*. It's a real book, bound with a spine, and with a picture of her on the cover, a picture of her smiling, not a care in the world, no idea what's in store for her. My poem is on page nineteen, which is a coincidence because that's the same day as my birthday. The book is for sale at the big book stores and online. The proceeds are going toward a new organization Leah's mother has started called *Leah's Wings* that will promote safety awareness to children across North America. It will focus on internet safety.

Mom and Dad were very proud to see my poem in the book, and I was too. When Mom looked my name up in the index and read the poem, she got tears in her eyes and had to excuse herself from the table so that Molly wouldn't see her crying. My name is right under the poem: Maxine Marie Lemay. For the first time ever, it looks like a pretty good name.

March 6

Dear Jo,

Today I showed *Leah's Book* to my therapist. She read the inside cover, all about how the book was raising money for *Leah's Wings*. After she read my poem, she told me it was great and that she was happy I'd found a way of getting my feelings out in such a mature and productive way, that it was sure to touch many people and make them think about life differently. I thought that was pretty neat, being able to make people see things in a new way. It felt good and powerful, and I said, "Maybe I should do more writing."

"Yes, you should. You seem to have a talent for it," she said.

"That's what Mr. Conroy told me too," I said.

"Well maybe that's your purpose, then. To write. To help people find a way to resolve the world around them, even if it's sad or scary."

"I'll give it a try," I said.

Then we talked about *Leah's Wings* and how Leah's mother was finding a way of resolving her anger, rather than just giving up. I know she was just trying to make her point, which was sort of irritating it was so obvious, but instead of getting angry, I smiled. If only she knew I had found a way to help, to *really* help. And yet, I couldn't tell her because I still can't tell anyone I was involved in the arrest, not even Lexi or Emma, not even Leah's parents, not yet.

March 19

Dear Jo,

Happy Birthday to me! I'm finally thirteen. Emma and Lexi and Kelsey and Amanda came over for pizza and cake, and we danced in the living room with my new Matchbox 20 CD turned up so loud, it probably rattled Mrs. Barnes's tea cups. Everyone was up dancing, even Mom and Dad, even Molly and Gus. I got all sorts of great presents, but my favorite is the new Avril Lavigne CD Detective Lucas sent me, which I thought was really sweet. The card was signed by all the detectives in his division.

I finally introduced everyone to Finn today, and they adored him as much as I do. Emma said she couldn't believe I'd had him for so long without inviting her over to see him. I said we were taking some time to get to know each other first. He's like my best friend now, and I feel that if anyone understands me, he does. Lexi said he was the nicest dog she'd ever met and that he was always welcome at her house. Then she said it was good to have me back. I knew what she meant, even though I haven't really been away anywhere.

I thought it was going to be a rotten birthday, but it wasn't. I mean, I didn't think I'd find a way to enjoy even a minute of my day without Leah to share it with. But I did. The first thing I did when I woke up was take down the birthday fairy she'd given me three years ago, open it with the silver key from around my neck, and re-read her letter. I hadn't read it in ages because I couldn't face it. And it's odd, but it felt as if Leah had written that letter especially for me to read today. The last paragraph said: *You are always a good friend and that is what is so special about you. Even when I act like a spoiled brat you still like me. I know you'd do anything for me and in case I don't say it enough, thank you for being my best friend ever. Love forever, Leah.*

March 22

Dear Jo,

I took Finn for a long walk around town today, mostly where I was sure I wouldn't see a lot of people. I walked through the neighborhood and to Lost Lake park where I sat and looked out at the lake. It was still early, so I didn't see many people on the streets. I was glad I didn't have to pretend I was going somewhere.

I was surprised to see that the snowbanks had melted away and the ground was bare. I hadn't even noticed the weather turn this year. In fact, I hadn't even noticed the leaves change in the fall or the summer flowers die, the sun start to go down earlier or the geese fly south, squawking as they flew over our house the way they do every fall. I've been so absorbed with everything, I've missed a lot of what's been going on – for one thing, Molly turned six in February and I forgot to mention it. She got a new velvet dress from Aunt Laurie, Walk-Your-Puppy Barbie from Granny, and a jewelry box that plays music when the lid opens from Mom and Dad. I hadn't gotten her anything, but Mom bought her a Bratz doll and wrapped it in pink sparkly paper and said it was from Gus and me. I felt guilty that I hadn't remembered, but she was happy with everything anyway. It's weird, because I've been spending more time at home with Molly and Gus and yet, I've been more out of touch with them too.

It was rare to see, but there was a merganser duck on the lake. I knew what it was because Dad and I saw a family of them skimming across the water a couple of years ago, and he told me what they were. They are strange little ducks with feathers that stick out the back of their heads, which makes them look like they have punk haircuts. This time, there was only one though. It was swimming around in small circles, as if it was searching for something. Sometimes it dove under the water and came popping up in a completely different place. I tried to guess where it would come up, but I could never tell, and it always surprised me. Once it was under so long, I worried something had happened to it. But then it came up right near the shore where I was sitting, and I jumped in my seat. It called out – made a strange croaking sound that echoed over the water. Nothing answered and it called out again. That call made me shiver. The park was mostly empty because it was early and cold and a little overcast. It was so different from the park the summer before last when

Leah and I spent the day and had a picnic on the raft, or from the park in December when we had the candlelight vigil. Today there was just Finn, the duck, and me, and I realized how the duck and I were the same, swimming alone in circles, calling out for an answer and never getting one.

March 23

Dear Jo,

I'm not sure why, but I've been feeling less tormented since 2funE has been locked up. I'm still not sleeping well, but I feel like the blackness is thinning a little, the way the sky lightens slowly at dawn and you know it's going to be a sunny day before too long. And I find myself drawn to writing in here more and more. In fact, sometimes during the day, I think of something to write down and can hardly wait to get home. Maybe the therapist was right and it does help to write things down. You feel like one of my friends now.

March 24

Dear Jo,

Detective Lucas called today to say that 2funE's

real name is Gabriel Basile. He has an apartment in the city, not far from where Aunt Laurie lives. They searched his computer and found all the e-mails he'd written to Leah and me and all those other girls. They also found a journal where he documented his various identities. I guess that's how he kept track of his lies. He was a freelance software developer, so he had strange hours and habits and spent a lot of time alone in his apartment. His neighbors said he was quiet and polite and are shocked that he could abduct and kill a young girl. They say that he just didn't seem like the type. But that's what people always say. You can't tell what a person is like by the way they look or by what they write on the internet.

They searched his apartment and collected all the evidence they needed to prove Leah was in his apartment. They did forensic tests, and even after all this time, they were able to find traces of blood and strands of Leah's hair. Detective Lucas says he must have driven her there after he picked her up in Port Hope, even though nobody in his building saw her arrive or leave or heard her scream. They don't know how long he kept her there before he killed her and drove her out to the forest to dump her body. But they were able to match his DNA to some on Leah's remains, so Detective Lucas says it's a done deal, that 2funE won't be free ever again.

March 25

Dear Jo,

I saw Gabriel Basile on the news tonight. He was sitting in a police car, surrounded by reporters and angry people who were yelling nasty things to him. He was in blue coveralls, and his hands were cuffed behind his back. He didn't even look sad about what he's done. I know I'm going to see his face and hear Leah's name a lot when the trial gets going, so I know I've got to come up with a way to stop imagining what he did to Leah and how scared she must have been, if she pleaded with him to let her go, and if she had any idea what was going to happen. She had to live through it once and it's over. I can't keep torturing myself by reliving it every day. I just can't let these thoughts go around and around in my mind for the rest of my life, or I will suffocate.

April 12

Dear Jo,

I'm sorry I haven't written in so long, but I've

been busy catching up. I have a tutor who's helping me with the schoolwork I let slide, and Mr. Conroy is letting me re-write the tests I failed. He thinks I have enough time, if I dedicate myself, to pass the year. I'm also trying to fit in time with Lexi and Emma and Kelsey and Amanda because when I opened my eyes and looked around finally, I realized they are hurting just as much as me, and that we need each other more than ever.

I was really depressed this past year. If I've learned anything, I've learned that depression is real and it's scary. It's like being someone else and out of control. But I'm glad to be back. Mom and Dad seem relieved, like I was when the duck came up from under the water finally. I think they're happy that I'm being more like myself lately, but I think they're suspicious too, waiting for me to spin down again. I don't think they're sure the "happy Max" will last. But it will. I'll be okay. I haven't forgotten about Leah, I never will, but like the therapist said, I can't forget about me either.

Tonight I've been re-reading a lot of the entries from the beginning, back in November and December when I first started to write, and you'll be happy to know that I've decided not to burn you after all. I can't, you're full of Leah and you're full of me. And I like us both too much to waste these thoughts.

April 13

Dear Jo,

Today I was outside playing in the mud puddles with Molly and Gus when Molly found a worm. She wanted to keep it as a pet, but when she took it inside, Dad told her she had to leave it in the garden or it would die. Molly said, "Will it go to heaven?"

"Of course," he said. "There's room enough in heaven for everyone and everything."

"So then can I take its body?"

I knew she was back to that whole topic about not being able to take your bones to heaven and that we were going to have to listen to her go on and on about it again. She's a lot like me – she just can't let a thing go once she gets started. At least she stopped having her imaginary friend, Georgia, around all the time. Mom says Molly has a memory like an elephant, which means it's good, I guess. In the end, she was okay about putting the worm back. She sang it a little song and said she would see it another day.

When I think back over the year and all about Molly's obsession with falling apart and her imaginary friend, I realize I wasn't the only person in this house affected by Leah's disappearance. It must have been hard on Molly too, suddenly not seeing Leah after seeing her almost every day for her whole life. I remember the first time Leah met Molly. Leah and I were only in grade one at the time and Leah couldn't wait to see her. She begged me every day for a month to invite her over to see the baby. When Molly started sleeping for a few hours at a time, Mom finally agreed to let me have Leah over for the afternoon. Unlike me, Leah loved babies. She was thrilled to hold Molly. She examined her little fingers and toes and sat with her in the rocking chair until Molly fell asleep. I remember being bored and wanting to go play – I wasn't at all excited about Molly being around and hogging all the attention. But Leah adored her and spent most of the afternoon hanging around Mom and Molly. When I complained to Leah about Molly later, she told me she wished she could have a baby sister, that I was the luckiest person she knew. She never really liked being an only child. She would have even been happy with Gus as a little brother.

April 15

Dear Jo,

Detective Lucas just called, and it was *soooo* good to hear his voice. I've really missed talking to him. We talked about school and Emma and Lexi and Amanda and Kelsey for a while, and he asked me how I was doing.

"I'm good. I've caught up on a lot of my school-work. I'm up to January. Mr. Conroy says I'll pass if I keep it up."

"That's good news."

"Yeah. I'd hate to fail the whole year. I want to be in class with all my friends next year."

"Guess what I bought today?"

"I dunno. A bag of gummy worms?"

He laughed. "No. *Leah's Book*. I read your poem. It's really good."

"Thanks."

"Will you sign my copy sometime?"

"Sure, I guess."

"I've never had a writer sign a book of mine before."

"I'm not really a writer."

"Sure you are. You have all sorts of hidden talents."

"Yeah? Like what else?"

"I bet you'd be a good public speaker."

"Me?"

"Sure. And I've got just the gig lined up for you."

"What do you mean?" I was a little suspicious.

"We're putting together a special show to go around to schools in order to let kids know about internet safety. Leah's mother is helping us fund it in your area. I thought maybe you could talk to the kids from first-hand experience, about how easy it is to get fooled. They'll pay more attention to you than they will to a bunch of adults."

"That's probably true."

"So are you in?"

"I guess. If my parents say it's okay."

"I'll call back tomorrow after you've had a chance to talk to them. Oh, and hey, are you available to look through some missing kids' Web sites with me sometime?"

"I dunno, why?"

"We're looking for someone with a good eye for detail and I think you'd be perfect."

"You mean you need me to crack another case for you?" I asked.

"Something like that. If your Mom says it's okay."

I was smiling so wide I couldn't speak.

Internet Safety Tips

Internet safety is a real concern, and internet predators are a real risk. A recent study by the National Center for Missing and Exploited Children in the USA found that one in five children have been sexually solicited online. Here are some tips for enjoying the internet and being safe at the same time.

When You're Online

- Never fill out questionnaires or any forms online or give out personal information (such as name, age, address, phone number, school, town, password, schedule) about yourself or anyone else. If you give your phone number to someone online, they can easily find your address and get a map to your house.

- Never agree to meet in person with anyone you have spoken to online.

- Never enter a chat room without a parent's presence or supervision. Some "kids" you meet in chat rooms may not really be kids; they may be adults with bad intentions. Remember, people may not be who they say they are.

- Never tell anyone online where you will be or what you will be doing.

- Never respond to or send an e-mail to new people you meet online. Remember: It is okay not to answer every e-mail and instant message.

- Never go into a new online area without first getting permission from your parents.

- Never send a picture over the internet or via regular mail to anyone you've met on the internet.

- Never buy or order products online or give out any credit card information online.

- Never respond to any belligerent or suggestive contact or anything that makes you feel uncomfortable. End such an experience by logging off and telling your parents as soon as possible.

- If you notice a friend acting odd or being secretive about what she/he is doing on the internet, be a good friend and tell an adult you trust.

- Always tell someone you know about anything you saw, intentionally or unintentionally, that is upsetting. (Parents: It is better for your child's mental health to be able to discuss exposure to pornography than for it to become a dark and confusing secret.)

For Your Parents

- Keep the computer in the family room or another open area of your home and be aware of any other computers your child may be using.

- Have children use child-friendly search engines when completing homework.

- Children should not complete a profile for a service provider, and children's screennames should be nondescript so as not to identify that the user is a child or identify the gender of the child.

- Look into safeguarding programs or options your online service provider might offer. These may include monitoring or filtering capabilities.

- Talk to your child about what sites they visit, with whom they communicate, and who is on their buddy list. No software will ever be a substitute for being an active parent.

- If you suspect online "stalking" or sexual exploitation of a child, report it to your local law-enforcement agency.

Compiled with help from:

"Online Safety," Oprah.com,
http://www.oprah.com/presents/2005/predator/safety/safety_online.jhtml

"Safety Tips," The NetSmartz Workshop: Keeping Kids and Teens Safer on the Internet," http://www.netsmartz.org/safety/safetytips.htm

Stolen Voices
by Ellen Dee Davidson
ISBN: 978-1-897073-16-2

"... definitely a page-turner that will keep readers captivated from the start ..."
– *School Library Journal*

"Set in an intriguing fantasy world, Davidson tells a compelling story that will strike a chord with many readers – a person's struggle to define herself and courageously make a difference."
– *ForeWord*

"... the mood is effective and the conclusion satisfying."
– Pamela F. Service, author of *The Reluctant God*

Life in Noveskina is designed to be harmonious and conflict free. But fifteen-year-old Miri, daughter of two of the city's Important Officials, faces a shameful dilemma. She has matured with no clear Talent and thus faces life among the lower classes. As Miri is confronted with the dark secrets of Noveskina, the quiet peace of her once-perfect world reveals itself as something infinitely more sinister.

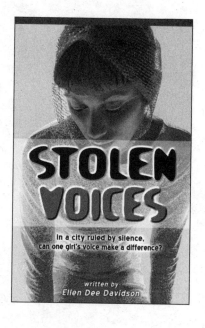

STOLEN VOICES

In a city ruled by silence, can one girl's voice make a difference?

written by
Ellen Dee Davidson

www.lobsterpress.com